Wands Up

Stars Hollow Paranormal Mysteries

Book 1

Giselle Jeffries Schneider

Kindle Direct Publishing

This is a work of fiction. Names, characters, places, and incidents either are the product of the author's imagination or are used fictitiously. Any resemblance to actual person, living or dead, business establishments, events, or locales are also used fictitiously. None of this is meant to be a biography or nonfiction.

All right reserved. No part of this publication may be reproduced, scanned, or distributed in any printed or electronic form without permission. Please do not participate in or encourage piracy of copyrighted materials in violation of the author's rights. Purchase only authorized editions.

Copyright © Giselle Jeffries Schneider
First Published in 2020

Published by Giselle Jeffries Schneider through Kindle Direct Publishing

Author: Schneider, Giselle Jeffries
Title: Wands Upon a Time

Note to Readers

Robyn Salem is on the autism spectrum. In fact, she is based on me. My own life and backstory have been used to create hers. With that said, remember that when you have met one person with autism, you have met one person with autism. We are not all alike. We are unique.

I also want to add that truth is stranger than fiction. Yes, this series *is* fiction/fantasy and most of it is a creation of my imagination, but some of what you will read is based on actual events I experienced.

I hope you enjoy the series.

Table of Contents

Copyright ii

Note to Readers iii

One of Those Small Towns 1

A Man with an Envelope 16

Not a Dream 28

Books, Satchels, and Potions 42

Lunch Magic 52

The Lockdown Spell 65

Stonewall Manor 78

Equality 93

For Good of All 107

Team Paranormal 116

They Walked into a Park 135

Emotions 145

Demon Section 158

Dead Men Tell Tales 175

To Keep a Secret 187

Pendulum 198

A Good Day Gone Wrong 210

Not Going to Let This Go 228

Amateur Sleuthing 239

Plans Unfurl 254

Epilogue 269

Other Publications.. 276

One of Those Small Towns

The sudden lack of that trundling sensation an old car makes is the first thing I notice. The second thing, the fact that I am rapidly slowing down despite having cruise control set. At first I think the control kicked itself off, so I push down on the accelerator to get myself back up to speed and prepare to set the control again.

Nothing.

This is the point my heart does two things at once – leaps into my throat and pounds like a stampede of horses.

My gaze shoots around, taking in the view from my side mirrors and rearview mirror. Surprisingly, no one is in sight. That is pretty strange for a busy freeway halfway between Twin Falls and Boise. I don't even see anyone coming from the other end of the divider.

I redirect to my mileage reader. I have gone down from eighty to sixty already. And here I notice that isn't all.

None of the lights on my dashboard are on. My car shut off.

I motion to turn the wheel and direct the car to the side in a panic, where my next revelation hits. The wheel barely rotates. It takes all I have to guide the car as the dial before me drops more and more. I am beginning to feel like I am on one of those teacup rides, and to my misfortune I have the one that refuses to cooperate. Even worse, I am afraid I will be stalled in the middle of the road, right in the way of future traffic.

Suddenly I have the image of bumper cars, but with real cars.

Then I am stopped. In the middle of nowhere. Luckily to the side, to my relief.

A deep sigh escapes, drawing attention to the fact I am trembling from the inside out. My heart is even still racing, and there is so much blood rushing through my head that I feel nauseous and ready to pass out. That is when I squeeze the steering wheel and drop my head against it and breathe in and out a few times.

Rush of moments like this get to me, forcing my blood pressure to rise and make me sick shortly after.

I turn to the tortoiseshell cat once calmed down enough, my forehead swiping against the hot, sweaty steering wheel. She is sitting in the carrier next to me, and it is turned so Coco can see me.

Coco meows that sound that is more like a cry and pants. I feel for her. It is hot, and my 1997 Chevy Blazer isn't blowing cold air, just air. But I do have the back windows down, not that having them down does anything.

I look back at Missy, the white cocker spaniel in the back seat who is fast asleep and oblivious, and wonder if leaving my parents had truly been a good idea. I could have let them continue treating me like garbage because at least I would have somewhere to live. At least I would have food and air conditioning. At least my pets wouldn't be overheating with no clue they may not have food a month from now.

I am so stupid, I tell myself mentally, making sure to put an emphasis on *stupid. Who cares if my parents beat me and find new ways to tell me how worthless I am? Who cares if I fear falling asleep at night because my mom might strangle me? Who cares if I flinch every time they move suddenly? And who cares that they frown on me being a writer and a substitute teacher so much they forced me into real estate, the worst job in the universe for someone like me?*

Again I take in the empty road around me, except this time I open the door and step out. Then I reach into the door compartment for the leash and groan when my muscles try to fight me.

Missy's hustle to get up is heard here and she appears in the driver's seat with barely a struggle.

"Come on," I say as I clip on the leash. There is no turning back now, and I think about my father's belt whipping me across the back a dozen times. Or his hand coming across my face and sending me into the wall or down the stairs. My father sent Missy into the wall a few times as I screamed for him to stop.

I flinch without meaning to.

Missy hops down and I reach across for the cat carrier.

Coco meows again and continues to pant. That worries me. She had been meowing up a storm for the first thirty minutes of the ride, the next thirty minutes had been pretty quiet. Now she just meows when she notices me noticing her.

I use my rear to close the door and walk to the back. I have some of those square blue ice packs. I figure if I stuff them all into the carrier, maybe it will cool her down.

Coco meows her cry again, and that persistence to be let out that I thought long gone resumes.

"Just hold on," I say. With that I set her on the pavement.

A car blows by and I hear my own car creak as it sways against the force of the wind. It is enough to push me sideways.

"Jerk," I breathe as I lift up the back door and open the small cooler. It holds only six water bottles and four of the blue ice packs.

Another car blows by and I grip the car as both

me and it sway. It is there I let myself glance out the front to see the back of a black SUV. Two cars now and neither bothered to see if I am all right. They didn't even switch lanes.

Coco's meowing brings me back to the cooler and I pull out those four ice packs. The water doesn't need them. From there I open the top of the carrier at my feet, Missy coming in to check out what I am doing, and I stick them along the sides. I grab two waters while I am at this and stick them in next to Coco as well.

But then I think we all may need more than two bottles of water and grab two more.

Finally, I close the back and head around to the front with cat and dog once more to lock the car. Old cars don't have those fancy key fob thingies... At least not mine.

I sigh again, look across what very well appears to be a very unforgiving road surrounded by farming fields. There isn't a house or town in sight. Yet as memory recalls, there is a sign for a place not too far away. Maybe the town isn't far, either, and I just can't see it from the road.

A glance at my watch tells me it is 7:15pm. So no

time to waste.

~*~

The individual letters to a town called Stars Hollow hang what appears to be in midair, high enough to sit in the first colors of sunset. It is like magic and art all in one. I literally can't see the wires that hold them up, or even what the wires would be attached to. It makes my jaw drop just looking at them.

And something about the name – Stars Hollow. It sounds so, I don't know… mystical. No, witchy.

I pass under the sign and trudge my way into civilization at last. It took an hour and forty-five minutes to get here under a blazing sun that refused to die out for the day, and many times I stopped to check on Coco and Missy. I personally feel ready to drop, and cry. Maybe it would be better if I just gave out right here and let the earth have me. This entire endeavor to find my own life and get away from my abusive family has turned into a nightmare.

Coco's newfound meowing, however, and Missy's heavy panting, keeps me going. They let me know they still live, and that I have a goal in mind. Besides, I found the town.

"Who is that?" someone whispers. A woman. "Is someone actually walking into Stars Hollow?"

"I can't recall ever having tourists or visitors," another woman responds. "My parents even said they never recalled anyone coming or going from this place."

Those comments confuse me, and I lift Coco into both my arms just to have something to do. She is also awkward to carry one handed as she is a rather large cat in a rather large carrier, and from there the loop to Missy's leash slides to my elbow. With that I glance sideways in the direction of the speakers to find a combination grocery and gas station. The building is small, doesn't even have much of a parking lot, and I catch the name.

OneStop.

That definitely says it all if it isn't already obvious.

Next, two women slip through my sight. They are out front of the store, and the moment we all see each other they spin around and dart through a set of manual glass doors. One of the women immediately reaches into her purse and pulls out a smartphone, the other is already texting wildly from a phone she had been holding the entire time.

I wish I had a phone, I think to myself. I had to leave mine behind because it was on my mother's plan, and she always threatened to shut it off if I didn't do as requested.

My feet turn to make their way over, but oddly they redirect as if they have a mind of their own. I end up going the opposite direction, almost as if I am trying to get away.

Odd, right?

Okay, maybe it isn't odd. Those women just don't seem the type to be helpful. And what could some small-town grocery/gas station do for me? I am not out of gas. I need a mechanic. A tow truck even.

A bell, like one you would hear over a shop door, chimes as I decide to go right down a street with my gaze following a path I could have taken. The town seems to be a maze, yet one that no one could get lost in as all roads eventually meet up. I see a diner called My Father's Place; a coffeehouse with doughnuts cutely named The Magic Brew, which sits funnily enough next to a pagan store dubbed The Apothecary. There is an old-style brick library under a clocktower, an antique shop and bookstore, a park with a gazebo. I note a courthouse.

I am entering the middle of a cozy little town.

Whispering, and it occurs to me there are eyes watching. Many eyes.

I stop. I shouldn't because some horror movie I am sure exists out there is racing through my mind. You know the one. The one where you realize you are being followed, then you turn around to find a horde of zombies or a town of cannibals licking their lips as they tauntingly play with whatever weapon of their choosing.

This is when Missy starts barking. Her leash jerks me forward before I know what hits me, and Coco's carrier fumbles and I nearly drop her.

Now I notice the people at every corner, standing in doorways, peeking through windows. This is one of *those* small towns. So cozy that everyone is in everyone's business.

"Missy," I hiss, regaining my balance and letting Coco slide back into one hand. Then I properly grab a hold of Missy's leash and attempt to restrain her.

Missy keeps barking, though, and pulling. Everyone keeps watching.

"Hey," comes a friendly voice. This one male.

I snap to attention abruptly, Missy letting out a shriek of terror that makes me jump out of my skin. This is the sound she makes when finally confronted with what she is barking at, and she rushes to cower behind me.

"I'm sorry," the man continues, stepping out of the park. He is white. Very white. Like a vampire. And his hair is black, which match his eyes, and sits wild. He is thin and is somewhere around my age – twenty-five. At last we are face to face, and here he laughs and bends down, extending a hand to Missy.

Missy ceases, a calm rushes over the area, and the whispering from earlier is gone. The eyes are still there, though.

"I didn't mean to frighten your dog. Missy, is it? I heard you say her name."

His voice is like his appearance. Strange how that works. "Y-yes," I respond, beginning to tremble as I had earlier. Missy's terror is still ringing in my ears, and finally I take in the fact the man is dressed to play the very part he matches.

"Where is your car?" the man continues.

"What?" My eyebrows rise, but all the man does

is stare up at me from his knees as he pets my dog.

"And is that a cat you are carrying?" he points to the carrier.

"Um…"

Coco's meowing never ended. I just tuned it out at some point.

The man stands up, a smile spreading across his lips, and he laughs again. "I take it your car broke down and you walked from the freeway?"

"Yes." I nod. Then I gulp and lick my dry, chapped lips.

"My name is Jasper. Jasper Alastair." He makes a gesture with his head. "Come. I work at the mechanic shop. We can leave your pets there while we get your car."

I follow along without a second thought. It doesn't even occur to me I never gave him my name.

~*~

Jasper pulls the tow truck up front of an inn, car dropped off at the mechanic shop that also functions as a hardware store. It is the bed and breakfast type. You know, the kind that used to be a grand three-story house but has been redesigned for the hospitality business. It sits just outside of Stars Hollow, at the south end. It is a beautiful old Victorian model, which this town is full of. Loads of creative styles that can take your breath away. All of these homes encircle the main part of town, but this one – The Haunted Inn – sits alone surrounded by trees and a flower garden.

"Don't worry," Jasper says as he parks the tow truck and shuts it off, his headlights keeping the dark that has fallen temporarily lit up. "This place isn't actually haunted. The owner is just obsessed with ghosts." He hops out into the night, shoes hitting the ground hard, and makes his way around the front of the vehicle.

I follow, Missy in tow and Coco in my arms once more. They had both been fed food Jasper and his father keep on hand as they waited for me to return.

"I'll help you with your things," Jasper continues as he opens the back door on the passenger side before I can even try and grab my rolling suitcase, backpack, and small cooler. He stacks them neatly atop each other and leads the way onto a dimly lit porch that wraps around half the place in a wide circular manner.

"This is nice of you," I comment. I honestly haven't said much until now. I normally don't say much to anyone, even if I know them. Communication is more awkward than carrying Coco and trying to walk Missy at the same time.

"Not a problem. Just one question…" He opens the door and steps aside. He smiles that smile again, and his hair flops into his eyes. "What is your name? You know mine, but I don't know yours."

I blush. Now that is embarrassing. I look down at the carrier I am holding, and Coco meows just once as she stares up at me through the bars of the top door. "I'm sorry. My name is Robyn. With a *y*."

A deep inhalation from Jasper. I spy up. We are still outside, under the light of the porch, and Jasper is still holding the door. "Well, Robyn with a *y*, is there a last name that goes with that? Just for my records."

"Salem."

That smile of his vanishes. "Salem?" His tone sounds, I don't know… shocked? His features shift like he is thinking.

"Uh…" *I bet he is confused.* At least he isn't making fun of my name, though. You have no idea how many times I was made fun of growing up for my name being the same as the one in connection to the witch trials. "Not the town. Spelled the same, but…"

His smile returns, interrupting me. "Gotcha." He gestures inside. "Ladies first."

I blush further, unsure how to respond from there, and step into an entryway set up as a waiting room with a couch, an armchair, and a table. There is a set of stairs rounding off to the immediate left and an open parlor to the right.

"It is straight ahead," Jasper comments as he clicks the door closed in his wake.

The next room, as I observe along the way, is the same size as the entryway. The desk is visible straight off, but stepping across the threshold reveals a closed sitting room turned office and a dining room straight ahead. I assume the kitchen is beyond.

No one is present, and I quickly recall the first words I hear upon entering this town.

Why is there an inn if no one visits this place?

Jasper reaches across and rings a little brass bell, and immediately a woman pops out of the office with a woosh of her door.

A Man with an Envelope

"A ghost!" the woman squeals at a decibel that makes Missy yip once. Twice. She is a bushy-haired red head, and she holds a peculiar device similar to an old Nokia cellphone in the air. But the thing remains absolutely silent as she rushes it back and forth, up and down. She spins around here and there. Zeros flash across the screen as it comes in and out of view.

One of those ghost hunting devices, I think as I set Coco on the desk so I can just hold Missy's leash and be free to check-in and pay and stuff.

"Alyssa!" Jasper calls out, trying to get the

woman's attention as she moves toward the hallway and away from us. It is like she doesn't even know we are there.

The woman brushes the device just inches from the hallway wall. I can see a wall phone there. Yes, a wall phone. Cord and all. There the device, an EMF reader I recall hearing it called on a show once, goes off like an alarm system and a red light starts flashing off an antenna.

My lids go wide. That actually doesn't sound good at all, which explains why readings like that get such big hits on ghost hunting shows.

Jasper reaches forward again and rings the bell like a maniac, hand going a mile a minute. It makes Missy yip some more. But both the ringing, and my dog, aren't quite as high as the frequency of the alarm.

Alyssa brings down the device at last and looks over at us disappointingly. Her freckled face nearly glows in the dark of the hallway, as do her green eyes.

"That EMF reader," Jasper resumes, "only catches the radiation of the electronics in this place. The wall phone, the kitchen appliances, the electricity..."

"My cellphone," Alyssa finishes as she sadly

nods her head. "I know. I know."

"This place isn't haunted," Jasper states. "It may have too much radiation, but it isn't haunted."

The woman holds up a finger and makes an *ah ha* face. "There you are wrong. I live in this inn, remember? I have lived here my entire thirty years. I know and see all that goes on. And I have seen a ghost. I just need to prove it."

"What you have seen," Jasper continues to argue, leaning into the desk, "is one of the Smith boys messing around. Possibly all three of them. They know you are a…"

Alyssa's finger comes back up, this time threateningly. "Don't you say it."

Jasper air quotes, "paranormal investigator."

The finger comes down, but it is replaced with a glare of emerald fire. "One day, you will see. This entire town will see." Then she turns to me and I almost step back as my lids go wider. "Did you know the second witch trials happened here? It was back in 1889. There was a witch by the name of…"

Throat clearing. A man. Except it isn't Jasper.

I rotate, looking to see who else is present. I don't

recall seeing anyone else. And my gaze lands on a man who... forgive my cliché... looks like a portly, round wizard. He even has the long white beard and hair. I quickly cover my mouth to keep from giggling, only I am sure my amusement is written all over my face and reaches clear into my eyes.

"Are you Robyn Salem?" the wizard man asks, in a very wizardly voice that makes me think of Merlin.

"Wait, you're..." Alyssa resumes behind me, but she is interrupted by the wizard man's hand.

Then silence as we all stand there, the three of us and the wizard man separated by the open doorway between entryway and reception desk. I remember I was asked a question.

"Yes," I venture, my hand coming down as naturally as I can make it. But then a nervousness rises as I imagine my parents, particularly my mother, hunting me down and claiming I stole my abuelita's wedding ring. She might be trying to have me arrested just to spite me. "I am Robyn Salem."

The man nods, reaches into the folds of his waist coat, which looks more wizardly on him than it does business, and he pulls out a thick manilla envelope. The really large kind. "Then this is for you."

I turn to Jasper, like he will tell me what to do. I don't know the man, just met him and all, but so far I am comfortable with him.

I am not comfortable with anyone.

Jasper shrugs. "This is Athanasius. He owns Broomstick Books and Antiques." He shows no concern or curiosity as he says that.

Oh, I think, glad I am not being arrested. Yet if I were, it should be for taking Missy. I have to admit, I stole my own dog. My mother admitted many times I could leave as long as Missy stayed. From there I step forward and reach out for the envelope.

"It would be best if you open it in private. Also, there is a house."

I take the envelope and turn it over in my hands. It is weighted, some areas more so than others, and my name is written in calligraphy across the front. "A house?" I echo. There I shoot my gaze across at Athanasius quick as lightning. It finally clicks, and I gasp. "A house?" I blurt this time. Just like that I hand back the envelope. "I think you have the wrong Robyn Salem. I…"

The wizard man raises both palms and shakes his head. "Nope. I have the correct person. You match the description perfectly. Down to your attire and pets."

"But…" I try to argue, except it is hard to with his statement.

"It is all yours. Everything in that envelope…" He indicates the item still in my possession. "And the house. I have everything set up for you. You are good to move in tonight. I can take you there myself if you like. I can give you a tour of the house."

I glance over my shoulder at Jasper, who is leaned backward against the desk, and he raises a brow that quickly vanishes under his dark hair. Alyssa has a studious expression on her face just beyond him as she observes each of us. He is realizing what I am asking so silently, and I note he is rather tall to be able to lean back the way he is.

"I can go along," Jasper finally answers. "I will help with your things." And he grabs the stuff he set off to the side.

~*~

The house, a Victorian, of course, that appears far more historic than the ones I have seen so far, sits to the upper west side near the entrance of town. Just beyond the cluster of neighborhoods. It almost sits alone, a gloomy cemetery separating it from the rest of the area. Its porch light is bright, and many little lights line the looping driveway like fireflies.

"This house has been vacant since June 5th, 1889," Athanasius begins to explain as we take on the surprisingly sturdy steps onto the porch. The porch is wide and looks to wrap around the entire structure unlike with The Haunted Inn. There is a porch swing and a small side table. "My family has had it in their possession until tonight, when I transferred all documents over to you."

Athanasius moves to messing around in his pocket here and pulls out a small keychain with a few brand-new keys, and Jasper and I halt behind him to wait. I desire to ask if this place has a connection to the story Alyssa almost ranted over, but something tells me I most likely won't get a proper answer out of these guys.

"Did you say June 5th, 1889?" Jasper askes to my astonishment, though, and I direct a baffled look his way.

"Mhm. That is correct."

The keys jingle in the new locks. There are two

sets to go through, one a dead bolt. Then the door opens. The entryway light is already on, and a quick look reveals new dark wood blinds closed tightly shut.

"Today is June 5th. June 5th, 2014 to be exact."

"Hmm," Athanasius hums as he looks up into the roof of the porch in thought.

I realize that is one hundred and twenty-five years. No one has lived in this house for one hundred and twenty-five years.

"You are correct, young man. Today is June 5th." He steps inside with that. "Now, all the electricity is updated to code, as is the plumbing. The yard has a sprinkler system and the back door has an electronic dog door. The gate to the backyard is locked from the inside and is located to the left of the house."

My mind goes into that numb state it is used to when I go on house showings with my mother. Or at least the way it used to. I am not a realtor anymore. I quit so I could stop wishing myself dead every day.

Athanasius' mumbling and drowning continues on as I venture behind him and Jasper from the entryway to the living space directly to the left. Someone flicks the lights on without question, and I rotate around to take in the fireplace with mantel, the antique furniture, the full wall nook of strange artifacts, and the naturally freshly painted walls. I breathe it all in, loving every bit of what I am seeing. This place holds its vintage style despite the upgrades.

"Now the room across from here is the dining," I catch wizard man say. His name is truly a mouthful.

I tag along, and I almost forget how to breathe when the lights flick on in this next destination.

The table. Oh my, the table. And the fancy dish cupboard with glass doors. Everything in dark cherry wood, and the legs of the table resemble lion paws.

Coco meows, and I remember I am still holding her and Missy.

"I closed the door," Jasper states. "You can let them loose."

I nod, setting the carrier down by the open doorway and handing Jasper Missy. I open the front gate this time, but Coco doesn't move. That is fine. Most likely she will sneak out when no one is looking and hide. Coco is my scaredy-cat. She is afraid of everything, except fireworks.

"Are their bowls and food in your bag," Jasper

continues. "I can give them water while you look around.

"Yes. Bottom pocket."

I catch Jasper go to that pocket as I hesitantly follow the rambling wizard man back out into the hallway and to the right.

"Kitchen is to the left."

I peek inside, and everything is stainless steel and marble.

"It had to be completely remodeled after the fire a decade ago. Then there are the stairs to the right. All the bedrooms and bathrooms are upstairs, although there is a half bath and laundry room along this hallway."

I nod and take on the stairs. I heard older homes usually have all the bedrooms upstairs and all the social rooms on the main floor.

"I hope you realize she is ignoring you, Athanasius."

"I catch little bits," I respond, blushing to the point I feel the heat in my spine. "I don't mean to not listen. It's just…"

"I understand," wizard man responds. "If I hated real estate, I would ignore me, too."

I ignore that comment intentionally. This

Athanasius seems to know everything about me. And at last I emerge onto another hallway, this time with the men behind me, to find a master bedroom facing the front of the house and three standard bedrooms with a shared bathroom facing the back of the house. There is a sitting room between them all, sliding doors left open to admire the comfortable furnishings and bay window.

"Is there anything still owed on this house?" I inquire now that I have processed what has been given to me. No one has said if this place was paid off before the last owner died. "Do I owe *you* anything?" And there is the caretaker thing, too.

"You own it outright. This property was willed to my family with strict instructions to pass it to you and no one else. We were always close friends, so we were happy to help."

I suck in my lips and squish them tight, then make my way to the master bedroom. I am determined not to inquire about how someone over one hundred years ago could see me coming.

"By the way," wizard man resumes. "You will find the deed to this house and the land in your envelope."

I look down at the item briefly as I step into what would be my bedroom.

"The envelope also contains your new bank account information, which I set up first thing this morning. You have five million dollars inside."

My heart stops and the envelope falls to the floor with a thump.

"It is all money that has accumulated over the years."

I blink, an amazing bed with the same lion paw legs in dark cherry barely making it into my view. Matching nightstands sit to both ends. Instead of a closet there is an armoire.

"I set you up with your own phone plan, too, so there is a smartphone and tablet for you in the envelope."

I look down at my feet, where I dropped the envelope with the two fragile electronics inside.

"They are boxed," Athanasius adds, like he could read my mind.

I bend down and pick up the envelope, then I turn back to the two men. "Five million dollars?" I say, the phone and tablet, which are all mine, still lingering in shock in my brain.

Not a Dream

A squeaky meow. Coco paws at the comforter by my face, her whiskers brush my nose. I flinch and jerk backward.

Every morning. She never fails.

I roll over, shoving my blue weighted blanket with black paw prints violently about to get comfortable. All the while my mind goes to that dream; that unbelievable moment where I have the courage to run away, and then things get weird.

Running away isn't possible, though. I don't make enough money to pay for rent or a house, and being a substitute I am out of work for two to three months every year. There is no holiday pay, no sick pay, no health insurance. Real estate is even worse, particularly next to my mother who claims I am stealing her money and ruining her life even though she is the one who gave me no choice in the matter after I graduated. I do all the paperwork and filing, by the way. My mother wouldn't know what to do without me as at her old company the assistant did the paperwork and filing (this new place doesn't allow that).

Of course, going bankrupt doesn't help as much as expected. I thought it would. You see, my mother guilted me into letting her use my credit cards, and then open store ones just for her to use with the promise of paying them off.

Yeah, right. Like she can even pay off her own bills.

I wish being an author would take off. I wish having a master's degree meant something. I wish every college/university teaching job I applied for didn't require twelve years of experience.

I pull my weighted blanket up to my nose, working not to cry. If I had at least one friend, maybe there would be a chance. One would think, being twenty-five, I would have at least one close friend who would say, "Hey, come live with me".

I swipe my face, my skin brushing along the comforter as it slips out from under the weighted blanket, and I pause.

Coco meows again and gets in front of me, where she begins pawing away at the comforter all over again.

Only the comforter is white. It is big, heavy, and thick, like hotel ones. Like the one I fell asleep under in my dream. It makes me feel like a princess.

That gets me to bolt up, and Coco darts away. There I look around at my grand master bedroom that can only be found in an old, historic Victorian house with all the updated accessories.

The day before, the evening, the night, hadn't been a dream.

I actually did it then, my mind processes slowly. From there I whisper it, like speaking the words will fully verify the situation. "I did it." My eyes rove around next, taking in everything in the new morning light, fingers grasping the bedding just to feel the fabric. Then I squeal, kick about until my weighted blanket thumps aside. "I did it!" I let out in a scream. "I am free!"

Patted feet scurry up the stairs in the near distance, the sound of them tripping drifts across just over my glee, and Missy bounds her way into the room in seconds. She is on the bed just as fast and up in my face with her stub of a tail sending her rear wagging instead.

"We did it Missy!" I squeal louder, grabbing her head and giving her a good pet.

Missy yips and playfully nips at my face.

"No more evil lady chasing you with a knife! Or horrible man kicking you into the wall!"

~*~

A calm after a rush of excitement, after realizing a major life changing accomplishment, is nearly impossible to obtain. I squeal again, for likely the hundredth time, in the middle of pulling on my knee-length blue jean shorts and I fall over. I hit the hardwood floor pretty hard, but I just laugh and get back up so I can grab a light green tank top and one of those frilly vest thingies. Last are my socks and black with tie-dye Sketchers.

Plus my fanny pack because I hate purses. There

are button pins all over it.

Coco slips back into the room at this point with one goal in mind, and she arches her body as she walks around my legs and meows.

I step over my cat and exit the room, Coco following me like a second shadow. My stomach is growling and demanding breakfast, and I need to check to see if Coco's auto feeder and waterer had been completely filled last night. I also need to feed Missy.

It is hard not to slow my pace and take in the part of the house I am in, though. To rotate a couple times to check if my new room is still there and not about to disappear and leave me stranded in some dream hallway. All of this is still surreal.

Then halfway down the hallway to take in the sitting room on my right and bedrooms straight ahead… or rather just short of that… my eyes catch sight of a long white string of web. The thing dangles between me and the stairs. The spider at the end is so big I can see it staring at me and taunting me.

I shiver. I hate spiders.

My stomach growls some more, but now in a sound that I swear vibrates off the walls. I remember I haven't eaten a thing since breakfast yesterday, and Coco is back to arching her way around my legs. That tail of hers wraps around me as she goes.

Apparently I stopped.

I encourage myself to move closer to my tiny enemy, step toward the side to squeeze around. There is actually loads of space, but it appears like a lot less with a spider dangling there in the way.

The string of web drifts by, and I stop a second time as my eyes focus in on the dangling arachnid just feet away.

Only it isn't a web, and the thing at the end isn't a spider. It is a cord and beaded handle.

My attention drifts up to follow the string to its end, my entire head tilting back, and I see a trap door in the ceiling.

"Was that there before?" I ask to no one. It is super weird I didn't notice a string dangling in the middle of the hallway before now. I should have run into it or bumped it. Jasper and Athanasius should have even seen it. Athanasius in specific should have known about the trap door.

I grab the string, thinking all these things over

and over because I just can't let them drop. I can't let the idea that this could still be a dream drop, which is how I kill my excitement. *It is very possible*, I ponder, pulling the string, *to have a dream within a dream*. So like dreaming, going to bed, and then waking up still in the dream.

The trap door drops, laying out a set of stairs before me.

An attic. I always loved the idea of an attic, although I never had one.

I make my way up them, my growling stomach an afterthought, and emerge into a wall to ceiling library shaped like the inside of a turret. I do vaguely recall a castle turret to the left side of the house. One large round window reveals the view from out front, the cemetery beyond. It is beautiful with the trees and flowers. A piece of the driveway can be seen, although there is no garage at the end of it. The driveway just loops around and goes back out.

I take the last step, breathing in dust as I do so. Dust that lingers on the air as I can see it shimmering in the light. Athanasius and his family may have owned this place for some time, but apparently this attic had gone overlooked. Can't blame them, however, considering *I* didn't even see the trap door cord.

The shelves on the right are the closest, so I go there first. There I am stricken by two things. First, the books are clean. Spotless. The shelf is dusty... oddly. Second, the books to this end are mine. Literally.

I pull down a book, a Tamora Pierce book, just to make sure I am not confused or imagining things. I open to the cover page and see, in purple ink, the author's signature. I put the book back and grab another, one I wrote in. All my notes are in the margins, my underlining is all there, my dog-eared pages are still firmly pressed down. A glance over reveals my Harry Potter set.

Now I know how old-fashioned women always feel faint. I think I am ready to do *that* right now as I set the book I am still holding back into place. But instead I run my fingers along the shelves, sending up more dust. I run my fingers along the books before I step away and tread dazedly along until I hit a part of the shelf that is filled with older books that I don't recognize.

My mind is trying to wrap around whether I am truly awake or asleep now. I thought I was asleep, then awake, now I am not so sure.

I walk away from the books to this end and move toward the other side, only I halt halfway at the sight of a podium. There is no book on it, or any papers. It is just an old, dusty podium, and the light hits it perfectly. I can see knotted designs along the stand and base.

That light also hits a trunk sitting under the window.

With a glance over at the unknown, leather-bound books along the rest of the shelves (they actually take up a good majority of the room), I make my way over to the trunk. I can tell straight away it has a lock on it, so I am not sure I will be able to get it open.

I bend down once I approach and swipe the dust off the lid.

Bad idea.

I breathe in every single particle and begin coughing. Although now I can see a Celtic symbol on the trunk. I know it is Celtic because it contains those complex knots and weaves and it looks cool, and this one I know specifically. It is a Celtic Shield Knot for protection and warding.

I stop coughing and touch the lock. It is built into the trunk and not one of those loose ones. It is also the kind that is hard to tell if it is locked. So I give it a go.

The lid opens and inside I find candles in an assortment of colors, dried herbs of all kinds, ready-made potions, empty potion bottles, ready-made satchels, empty satchels, and a massively large book. There is also a wand.

I reach inside, wondering how far a protection spell will allow a stranger to go, and my fingers grasp the smooth surface of the wand handle.

A spark, it tingles across each digit as I grasp the item and pull it out. Once I officially have it in my grasp, it just feels right. Like sunshine and flowers on my skin. And now that I have the wand in the open, I can see the twist of vines and leaves along its length. The wood is oak.

"Beautiful," I breathe.

That spark, like the wand can hear me and is accepting the complement.

A twitch of a smile escapes my lips, that excitement from earlier returning.

Then a rustle from behind.

I jolt, snap around to the point I smack my side and elbow into the trunk, and notice just in time a piece of yellowed paper flutter onto the podium.

~*~

My Dearest Robyn,

Let me begin by introducing myself. My name is Serina Salem, I am twenty-five-years-old, unmarried, and the current date is June 5th, 1889. I am the last of the Salem witch family here in Stars Hollow, or at least I will be soon.

That last bit is something personally hard for me to realize. You see, the Salem family is one of the four founding families (Salem, Stonewall, Thyme, and Cottonwood). Our blood literally runs through this town. We built it right under a cluster of stars, nourished it, made it a sanctuary for all magical beings and humans. This place is utopia, our little safe hollow to call home.

That is, until ten years ago.

This is a very long, complicated story, but basically I have a little sister. Her name is Agatha. Well ten years ago, Agatha turned to dark magic and married a demon from the Underworld. She brought this creature, who has to be the ghastliest being I have ever seen, to the surface. Now we are in the midst of a second witch hunt and the slaughtering of hundreds of innocent lives. People from all over the world are being murdered for being human, for being a witch, for being a shifter, for being anything. Fires are raging everywhere, the earth constantly shakes, the sky rains ash from grey masses that can't possibly be clouds...

I tried to stop her. Our entire family did. I am the only one left after all these years, and there is only one thing left I can do.

That brings me to today. I am writing this because tonight, or rather tomorrow morning, I must sacrifice my own life for the sake of the world. This means at exactly three in the morning and at the hands of the other three founding witch families and a wizard, silver athames anointed in moon water will be driven clean through my heart one at a time as each person gives a prayer to the goddess. My blood will spill across the center of town, spreading with it a spell that will strip Agatha and her children and their children's children of all they are and banish them.

From there, the monstrous demon will be sent back to the Underworld and a lockdown spell will be put into place. All who are human, whether they live here or outside, shall forget all that is magical. Even more, no one will be able to travel in or out and murder within Stars Hollow will no longer exist. Small crime will be possible as not all can be prevented, but murder or anything that physically harms an individual will be impossible. Think of this place becoming an actual utopia for magical beings, demons, and any humans who linger.

My life is a small sacrifice to make. The pain I will endure a small ordeal. The love I gave up worth it. I would do it over and over again if I have to and wouldn't think twice. In fact, I will smile as I watch the stars return to the sky and smell the fresh new leaves.

I had a vision, however. This is the purpose for this letter. I had a vision that exactly one hundred and twenty-five years from now you will arrive in Stars Hollow and the lockdown spell will break. All will remember our town's existence (not the magic, although there will be hunters with strange devices), and you will reclaim what is rightfully yours.

You are a witch, Robyn. A very powerful witch. You are a Light Witch, but also a Dark Witch as you come from Agatha's line and carry a small amount of demon blood. Don't be frightened. You are not like her, not like that demon, and not like your mother or your father. You are not even like your siblings.

Yes, I know you, Robyn. I have seen your plight and who you have become despite it. So with that, protect Stars Hollow with your life. Don't let crime get a rise here, don't let humans know magic exists, and don't let a third witch hunt begin. This world will not survive a third war.

Athanasius is available for any questions. He is a wizard and has been a family friend for centuries. There is also his cat, Hawthorne, who is quite knowledgeable for a snarky white fluffball.

And before you think it, this is not a dream.

Yours truly,

Serina Salem

Books, Satchels, and Potions

The little bell above Broomstick Books and Antiques chimes, and the world goes from bright and wide open space to dim and cluttered. This shop is a hoarder's dream with antique furniture lined and stacked along one wall, décor bunched up along another, and shelves of books streaming into man-made paths all the way to the back.

"Athanasius?" I call out.

"I am over here!" he responds from what could very well be the world beyond.

My ears work to locate the direction of the voice,

my feet choosing a path to take, and I bump into a table. "Oops," I say as I catch the item before it topples, and I note sheets of paper written all over as though someone were researching.

"What is that?" Athanasius calls out.

My ears perk. "Sorry! Just bumped a table!" I keep going, avoiding open boxes of other strange antique items. Finally I make a turn left, sensing this to be the direction of Athanasius.

Something brushes against my legs, and I glance down as I maneuver to avoid stepping on whatever it is.

It is a cat. A fluffy white furball half the size of Coco, and he is purring up a storm. "You must be Hawthorne," I say, not sure if familiars talk. I am guessing he must be a familiar based on Serina's note about him. And I am guessing Athanasius was her lover.

"I am," Hawthorne responds with a silky, kittenish voice. He finds his way between my feet, halting me completely. "And you are going the wrong way, little witch. He is this way." With that he is sauntering off the opposite direction and turning before I can think twice.

"Hey, wait up!" I holler

Wands Upon a Time

"What is that?" Athanasius calls out again.

"Your cat!" I respond.

"Oh!"

I round that corner and spot Hawthorne's long white tail dance like a feather just as it rounds another corner.

Now this is a maze to get lost in.

"Keep up, little witch," Hawthorne calls back. "This place changes every day. Meaning a new maze to memorize every visit."

"Now that is not true," Athanasius responds, much closer now.

"With all the things you gather up…" Hawthorne rebukes, but he doesn't finish.

One more corner following that white tail and I reach the back of the shop, where Hawthorne immediately jumps onto a desk and wraps his tail around himself. The hair around his face poofs out like a lion's mane, and his blue eyes narrow in on me. The dang cat is still purring, too.

"You enjoyed that, didn't you?" I ask, giving him an insulted look even though I don't mean it.

"Yes." He proceeds to lick himself and swipe his

Wands Upon a Time

paw along his head and face, that purr intensifying.

There is just one thing missing. Athanasius.

"Hey!" I call out, scanning the area. This place seems the messiest with open books and paper everywhere. It is the work area of a scatterbrain.

"I am here, Robyn." And the portly, round wizard man slips out from a door to a storage room I did not see. He is holding a book open in his hands and is flipping pages quickly, pupils darting hither-tither. "I am sorry. I slipped back there real quick."

"That is all right." I take off my messenger bag with that and set it on the desk next to Hawthorne, who is now viciously cleaning his rear. "I have a few things I found that I am wondering if you can look at." I pull out three satchels first and a couple potion bottles.

Athanasius sets his book down, still open, and picks up a satchel. "Are these from that trunk in the attic?" He slips the draw strings apart and pulls the satchel open, where he peeks inside.

"Yes." I pull out my book next and the wand. Last is the note I slipped into a small interior pocket.

"I remember the day Selina made this. It was the day she..." He closed it up and set it aside without finishing the sentence. "It contains smokey quartz, rose quartz, peppermint, and lavender for social anxiety. She said you are the nervous type, particularly in social situations."

It felt like an eternity before I released the note and let it fall on my book. *Is it that obvious?*

Athanasius simply picks up the second satchel and peeks into that one. "This is for protection. It contains snowflake obsidian, quartz, basil, cinnamon, garlic, bay, mint, and cedar."

"I take it she was worried about me?" I ask.

"With your innocent nature, yes." He grabs the third satchel and peeks inside. "Aura protection. It has frankincense, myrrh, resin incense, rosemary, and yarrow. This one comes with a spell you will need to chant. In fact…" He scratches his forehead. "… so does the other protection satchel."

"Can you teach me them?" I ask shyly, not sure he even can considering he is a wizard and not a witch. I am actually not sure about the difference. Some people believe one is male and one is female, others believe they are completely different beings with similar magical skills. Some even think their abilities are completely different.

"I know the words, so I can. As for these…" He picks up the potions. "This blue one is to enhance intuition and this green one is for truth. Just sprits them in the air before the person intended. Do not drink or douse yourself in them."

"What happens if…"

"Things can get crazy fast," an unknown male voice responds.

I jump, quickly place myself in front of my things, and pretend to be confused as I come face to face with Thor, but with short hair. Thor is not good looking with short hair. He is also not good looking in black slacks and a blue polo shirt.

"Hello, I am Leo Stonewall," the man introduces himself, sliding up next to me as only a rich snob can.

"Robyn," I respond, quickly relaxing at the name and returning to my things.

He directs to Athanasius. "Do you have my mother's order? She needs it."

Athanasius raises a knowing finger, his face lighting up. "Yes. I do. In the back." He pats my hand by surprise, getting me to look down at where we both make contact. "Just hold tight, Robyn." And he trots off into the back room, which is funny to witness as the man's frame is not built for moving like that.

I shuffle my feet and readjust myself to lean against the desk, all the while trying not to look at this Leo Stonewall. The man turns out to be difficult to ignore when he begins to drum his fingers on the little bit of space before him, and I think he is staring at me. Then the guy goes and breathes a nasally sigh, and I twist away to find Hawthorne the one to be staring at me. No, glaring daggers at me.

"What?" I ask the cat. I don't mean to sound irritated, but it comes out that way. Next thing I know I am giving him an apologetic look.

"Pet me, witch."

I reach out to do just that, wondering if all cats think the same way.

Pet me, slave, or *Pet me, human.*

I make sure to start with the spots around those adorable ears and under his chin. His hair is mighty soft.

"That is not nice, Hawthorne," Leo intrudes. "Don't enable him, Robyn."

Hawthorne leans into my hand, front right paw

going up, and I see his eyes go into slits of enjoyment.

"Who is enabling?" Athanasius chimes in as he returns. But then… "Hawthorne!"

The cat jolts and darts off with a hiss.

"I really don't mind," I say, thinking of how Coco loves to be petted twenty-four/seven. She loves to be fed twenty-four/seven, too. "I love cats."

"That cat used to be a wizard," Athanasius replies, but he doesn't sound upset with me. His tone has gone back to normal. "Being a familiar is his punishment for breaking magical rules that harmed many people. Here, Leo." He passes off a rather large box. A smaller one atop it. "Let me know if there are any issues."

"I will. Thank you." He heads back out the way he came.

I grab my book from there and show it to Athanasius, slipping the letter off it so it doesn't get lost in the mess. It is in some weird language. I couldn't even find it in Google translate.

But before the wizard man could take the book…

"Oh, and Robyn?"

I twist around. The boxes seem to weigh nothing in Leo's arms as he stands halfway down the aisle of books and antiques, his arm muscles making his shirt sleeves tighten.

"My family invites you to dinner tonight. It is not an option. Wear a formal evening dress and bring your wand."

My jaw nearly drops. So demanding. He doesn't even ask if I am available to attend. Yet he doesn't seem to care as he simply resumes walking away just like that, leaving me staring until he is no longer in sight.

"His mother, Samantha, is mayor of Stars Hollow," Athanasius chirps up. "Richest family, too. They don't marry outside the witch line, although they are all for equality."

I return to my book, all sorts of sensations running through me. Not a single one pleasant. One for sure is annoyance, another nerves. "What if I don't want to go to dinner?" My eyes fall on the hard cover of my book here. This is the only book in all the magical ones in that attic not made of leather. It is imprinted with the symbol of a sun within a half-moon.

"I am afraid it does not appear to be an option," Athanasius echoes Leo as he takes my book from my grasp at last. "Also, Endora Stonewall is coven leader with Samantha and Darren next in line, so avoiding is probably not a wise idea if you wish to stay in town. But you do have your social anxiety satchel. Make sure to take it along with the other two."

I guess that is the best I can do, so I leave it at that.

"This is the Salem family grimoire," Athanasius proceeds, opening the book and flipping the pages. "It is in the Witch Language. There is a spell to help you read it, but you need a witch to cast it on you." That answers the question of whether witches and wizards are just gender names or different beings. So does the satchel spells, come to think of it. "I could teach you as I have spent time studying the language, but it could take years." He eyes me over the book here. "A good reason to have dinner with the Stonewalls."

I sigh. I really do hate gatherings, and I hate it even more when I am forced to attend. Even worse is when I don't know the people attending, or it is a business gathering or a party.

Parties suck.

"Now, for those satchel spells."

Lunch Magic

The bell chimes my exit of Broomstick Books and Antiques. It goes well with the afternoon as it lights up the town of Stars Hollow as if for the first time. I think I like the sound with the world opening up, too, over entering a small, cramped building.

    I glance across the road then, to the gazebo I learned from a particularly small map provided by Athanasius is the center of town. The beautiful white, ivy-covered piece covers the ritual circle in which Serina sacrificed herself. Where she remains buried. I wish to stand there for a bit and honor this ancestor I never knew.

Thank her for all she has given me.

Except I barely take one extra step toward my next destination when I collide into an unmovable force with an audible *oomph*.

Or the force collides into me. It is hard to say.

"Whoa there!" comes Jasper's voice.

I blush in a panic. I hate that as it rushes not just across my cheeks but through my nerves, too. I can feel it in my spine just like last night. "I am so sorry!" And I squint as I search for his face in the blinding light. I am sure my horror is very visible, too.

Jasper laughs, his amusement the first thing to greet me. "No worries."

I blush deeper, nonetheless, and make sure to stare at his mouth to avoid the overwhelming task of looking into his eyes. People just have so much in their eyes, and then I am directed to facial changes. I simply can't think straight when I make full eye contact, although I have done it – it is not impossible. But as I said, I can't think straight.

"So I am wondering if you would like to have lunch with me," Jasper proceeds.

That draws my attention upward, and my brown

eyes lock with his black ones unintentionally. There I gasp when I see him smiling clear across every visible feature, his eyes still laughing in amusement. At least, I hope it is amusement and not something worse. *Did he just* ask *to have lunch with me, not demand it?* But then I find I am not bothered by looking into his eyes, and I relax.

"The diner here is great." Jasper points with his thumb over his shoulder. "Sookie is a great chef. There are many different things on the menu. We can talk and get to know each other…" Jasper is rambling.

I know rambling. I do it, too, once I get to talking about something interesting.

Jasper's hands begin to move here, like mine get to doing, and they go wild under my vision. "I can show you around after. Just as friends, of course. It's not a date or anything."

I adjust my messenger bag just as it slides into an uncomfortable position against my side and I suck in a breath to respond. Lunch doesn't sound like a bad idea, and Jasper could show me where to shop for a dress.

"Unless you already ate, then…"

There my stomach growls, cutting him off. I

forgot to have breakfast. I forget breakfast a lot, sometimes lunch and dinner, too. It is really bad on reading and writing days. But I never forget to feed Coco and Missy.

Jasper smirks.

"I would like that," and I look around. I do recall a diner, and Jasper pointed in its general vicinity. Someplace called My Father's Place.

"Great. It is this way."

Before I know it, Jasper's hand is on my back and guiding me along the sidewalk. His touch doesn't seem to bother me, either, and I spot the sign for the diner immediately. The place is on the other side of Bejeweled, a clothing store. I wonder if this other place has dresses. This little strip only holds these two buildings and Athanasius'.

Jasper opens the door to My Father's Place and holds it open, another bell chiming. "Ladies first," he announces just as last night.

"Thank you." I step in.

The place holds ten small sixties-style tables placed randomly about. They are white with red. There is a bar to the left, that same sixties-style seating before it, with a swinging door to the kitchen. There is also a hallway to the back where I spot the restroom sign and a set of stairs. The windows have curtains only on the bottom half. A few customers are present other than us.

"I prefer the table over here," Jasper comments as he leads the way to a corner, just off to the right against a window.

I notice the few customers stop eating to watch us pass by. I wonder if they are human or magical. And if magical, what kind.

Jasper pulls out my seat, taking me aback. No one has done that for me before. "Sorry, too forward?" he asks, his face curious.

I shake my head. "No. Thank you." I sit and slip off my bag, which I set on the floor between me and the window, and I feel my wand poke me from behind. The magical item is slipped into my back pocket and hidden under my tank top. I decided to carry it where I could grab it, not that I know any spells or charms yet. "I like that you are such a gentleman." It is true. It honestly did simply take me aback.

He chuckles as he walks to the seat across from me. "Gentleman. Not many of those, I guess."

"No," I agree.

A man walks up to our table. The only thing to suggest he works here is the notepad and pencil in his hands as other than that he is dressed in a red flannel shirt rolled up to his elbows. The shirt works with his dark brown, almost black, skin, and it is tucked into his navy-blue jeans. He also wears a hat on backward. All his teeth show as he grins ear to ear. "This must be our new resident. Robyn, correct?" His voice has a soft deepness to it.

I nod. "Yes." It seems everyone knows me now, which is a little creepy since I haven't met more than three, four, people.

"My name is Sam. I own this diner. Would you like a menu or do you just want to know the specials for today?"

I purse my lips and look to Jasper.

"I honestly love their burgers," Jasper comments, sitting back. "I get the same thing for lunch every day. But Sookie also makes amazing pasta dishes, sandwiches, seafood."

"That my daughter does," Sam comments proudly. How nice to have a parent who is proud.

"Shrimp fettuccini?" I ask, looking up at the owner of the diner.

Sam writes that down. "And to drink?"

"Sprite."

"I will be back with your food." And he is gone.

"So how has your day been?" Jasper asks right off the bat.

I slip my palms between my knees and scrunch my shoulders close. I have to lie a bit. "Good. I found some antique books and took one to Athanasius to ask about it." That has a weird taste in my mouth – lying.

"Antique book?" Jasper raises a brow.

"Mhm. And some neat…" I raise a hand to indicate size. "… knick-knacks."

Both Jasper's eyebrows go up. "So an exciting day already. I am guessing it made you forget to eat."

I look out the window. The gazebo is within sight from this position. I shrug. "I would have remembered eventually." Most likely when I got into bed. I scan the grass with that, thinking of the letter, Serina's death and how Athanasius most likely held her as she took her last breath, and what Stars Hollow looked like in 1889.

"Penny for your thoughts," Jasper inquires

further. That is a phrase that makes no sense. A penny is useless.

But that directs my thoughts to an appropriate topic, which is how one of the people who helped Serina sacrifice herself was a Stonewall and now I have to have dinner with them. I bet they will invite all the founding witches, all of them connected to that sacrifice, just like my mother makes things family reunions at the last minute. "I am just wondering where to buy a formal dress here," I respond. "Leo Stonewall said his family requests I have dinner with them."

"Ah. I can show you after this. I actually have the day off, so…"

Jasper's words fade away with the trees. I am serious. The trees are dematerializing before me. My head tilts slightly as I watch them go one by one, glistening objects replacing them quickly. The gazebo is last.

I blink, straighten, and look around to find the diner is gone as well. Jasper is gone.

The glistening objects move in close, revealing a couple stoves, a few microwaves, loads of counter space with vegetables and other food items, dishes. I am sitting in the middle of a large kitchen. No, standing. I am holding a pan and a wooden spoon. I don't know how any of this is possible.

I turn, looking for someone. Anyone.

There is a clatter.

I spin back around and orange fills my sight with a roar. There is smoke. I smell a hint of something burning and scan for the source.

"Sookie! The towel!"

I note something grey turning black, things around it are singeing fast behind it.

Sam rushes into my sight in a blur of red and blue, then white sprays everywhere.

Except the orange grows into large flickering flames with the attempt to put it out. I can feel it on my skin now as the flames become defined, but I just duck out of the way and look down into alfredo sauce that smells amazing despite the terror around me. Despite the terror that is and is not in me.

I don't know how it is possible to be scared and not scared at the same time.

Then screaming. Several people are screaming.

There is an explosion. It fills my ears with ringing

as all goes dark.

"Hey!" Jasper's voice enters harsh, but gentle.

Snapping. I blink again, the dark vanishing just like that, and find Jasper waving in my face. The diner is once more all around me and Stars Hollow outside. My heart feels ten times its normal size as it beats against my chest, although I don't remember feeling it earlier.

"Everything all right?"

Before I can even process what to think or say, that clatter comes and I jump nearly out of my skin. It sends my heart going even faster until I am sure it is running somewhere without me.

"Sookie! The towel!"

My eyes go wide. Jasper before me looks worried. Serina had said she had a vision of me, which means…

"Robyn?" Jasper ventures cautiously.

"The kitchen!" I scream, and I am on my feet and running toward the bar. I slide around it and shove open the swinging door beyond.

Fire wafts across and licks my skin, and there the screams come early. But I keep going because the flames don't fill the kitchen entirely yet and it hasn't actually escaped out. It isn't too late. And it is also right there at my left, where Sam is hopelessly spraying it with a fire extinguisher.

I reach behind me for my wand, a voice whispers a word in my mind I won't remember until I hear it again, and I swish it out and repeat.

A burst of clear light spills from my wand and the fire goes out.

"Sookie!" Sam breathes in terror as he kneels on the floor, extinguisher dropping with a clank and rolling away.

There is a young woman with thick black hair under a purple bandana and a small brown face sitting against the stove. She is holding a pan of alfredo sauce and a wooden spoon. "I think I outdid myself," she giggles. There is no fear whatsoever in her voice. "Taste, daddy." She holds up the spoon, and Sam takes a taste.

"Yes dear, your best." Here Sam grabs her by the arms and helps her up. "But you need to be more careful. You almost took down the diner this time."

The rush hits there and I double over. Hands appear around me.

"Just breathe, Robyn," Jasper says behind me.

"Or maybe sit on the floor for a moment."

"I will get her water," Sam interjects.

I don't sit, but I do put my hands on my knees to help keep me up. And I notice my wand is still out, and I never recall the swinging door slapping shut behind me.

The water appears before me.

"Thank you, Robyn," Sam continues. "Sookie's magic gets away from her sometimes."

My head goes up and I meet Sam's relieved expression. "You are witches, too," I breathe in relief, surprise that words even come out at all.

"Yes. I guess you have no clue who is human and who isn't, huh?"

I shake my head and go down, hand going out for the glass, and I end up taking a spot against the stove. "I just reacted without thinking."

The water splashes over the rim and down my arms. I am trembling terribly.

"Here." Jasper takes control and helps me drink. "And by the way, I know about magic. But your lies earlier were pretty amusing, so thanks for that."

I splutter as I drink. I am embarrassing myself by the moment.

"Let's make this lunch on the house," Sam offers. "As a thank you for saving my diner. That fire just wasn't going out. A good conversation for dinner tonight with the Stonewalls, though."

I learn later Kitchen Witches are limited to kitchen and food magic. Although they can also do wand magic (Sam Thyme just doesn't have his on him at the moment), potions, satchels, pendulum rituals, and group rituals as those are standard magical tasks. Weather Witches and Earth Witches are in the same situation with their magical areas. Me... I can do anything from wand magic, spells, charms, curses, rituals of all kinds, candle magic, potions, talismans, satchels, and have the rare ability to see the future. I can even cross over into kitchen, weather, and earth magic with some of the things in the grimoire. I am basically an all-around witch.

The Lockdown Spell

"Soooo," Jasper draws out after five minutes of waiting for me outside the dressing room door, "how does the dress look?"

I purse at myself in the mirror as I take in the floor length dark green dress. The tag calls it a draped one shoulder mermaid evening gown. It looks nice on the manikin, but on me... "I think I look stuck up and snooty, like my Tia Consuela." I hate myself after saying that because that relative's name has always been used as a way to insult me. My parents claim I have the same brown hair, same shaped face, same thin body, same tan skin. Same crazy. I can actually see my Tia Consuela in the mirror now, wearing this dress with her nose in the air like she is the Queen of England.

Chuckling. "That's the most ridiculous thing I have ever heard. A dress doesn't make someone look stuck up and snooty. The person does that."

I rotate to see the back of the dress. I don't like how much skin it shows. And that hip thing, as well as the shoulder thing, that I think makes the company refer to it as mermaid are annoyingly in the way. "But it's true."

"Come out here and let me see," he responds with a notable smile.

I suck in a massively deep breath through my nose, puffing up my chest that I think makes the dress look worse because I am small breasted, and open the door.

Jasper's eyes go wide and his face does this contortion thing.

"See," I say, flipping the stupid mermaid hip thing, "horrible." And for some reason I think of that time my Tia Consuela bragged about buying incredibly torn jeans for a hundred and fifty dollars; they were all the rage, as she said.

Jasper's face softens right back up and he gestures to my hair. "Well with those double ponytails…"

I stop flipping the side of the dress and look over my shoulder into the mirror again.

"But if you don't like it. Try on one of the other two." His reflection looks back at me just as my own does.

I sigh and lock myself in the dressing room again. Then I grab one of the other dresses the store owner picked out (I never got her name) and give it a look. It is another floor length gown, but in purple with splashes of pink, no sleeves or straps, and a poof of frills at the bottom. There is no way that thing is staying on me even if I do consider it, so I set it on the reject side.

"You know," Jasper comments. "I think you are the first female I have met that doesn't like parties, dresses, trying on clothes, or shopping."

The last dress is in my hands in seconds. This one is actually my favorite. It starts out in midnight blue and turns into a medium blue. There are sparkles on the left side (the rib cage area) and sparkles on the one shoulder strap to the right. The back is a set of diagonal straps. It is fancy, yet simple at the same time.

"How is it you don't even own a dress?"

"The last dress I wore was a prom dress," I respond, slipping off the green dress and putting it back on the hanger for the reject side. "It was for a senior prom I didn't even want to go to, my dad was my date. It still fit, but I didn't have space in my suitcase so I left it behind."

"I see. So how is this other dress?"

"Hold on." I snag the nice blue one back up and roll it up, prepare it to go over my head, and swoop myself under. I can't help but see how wonderful it looks as the fabric slides down to my toes.

"Can I see now?" Jasper presses further. "I am sure one of them has to be perfect for you."

I open the door again and step out, my joy on my face.

Jasper's features do that contortion thing again as his eyes once more go wide. "Wow," he breathes. "You were right before. The first was hideous. I think this is the one. Make sure to wear your hair down, though. And no makeup; you look perfect and brilliant with no makeup."

As I did before, I look over my shoulder at my reflection. The straps on the back cover more than the nothing on the green dress. And there is no funny mermaid tail hanging down my shoulder or over my hip. Plus, no poof or frills or feathers or whatever else comes on absurd dresses. "I agree."

I swear my eyes shimmer along with the sparkles on the dress as I smile.

~*~

Jasper and I stop on the sidewalk for me to readjust the dress bag over my arm and against my messenger bag. The dress is awkward with a small matching draw string purse and wedges hanging along with it and weighing it funny. Now the shoes are an understandable addition I agreed to without argument, but Jasper had to convince me to get the purse.

"The purse can hold your..." He had dropped to a whisper and leaned in as he spied around the shop. "...satchels and wand."

I reluctantly agreed, but I don't look forward to carrying the accessory or trying to remember to set it where I can see it.

"So I think we should stop one more place before we finish up," Jasper comments after a time.

I straighten and take in the small town, not sure where else I would need to go. Everyone else seems to enjoy going here and there, though, because the entire town is out and about. Chitchat hums in the air.

"You see," Jasper explains, "your car is done for."

That gets my attention back on him. I forgot about my car, and for a brief moment I also forgot I have five million dollars now. I take a mental note to pay off my sixty-five-thousand-dollar student loan debt once I get home. Can't go bankrupt on student loans.

Jasper, however, looks guilty as he proceeds. "My dad and I tried to figure out a plan to fix it, but it would honestly be better to buy a new one. I know some people are attached to old cars, but sometimes…"

I realize where this is going and give him a wave, cutting him off. "The car doesn't mean anything to me, and I am not an old car hoarder." That gets me to thinking of the day I finally got my own car, though. "My parents bought it for me used my senior year of high school. It took me ages to convince them my sister's hand-me-down Tracker was a piece of junk and kept shutting off at traffic lights."

With a tilt of his head, Jasper takes me in slowly. "So your parents gave you a hand-me-down piece of junk and then a new piece of junk?"

I shrug. I never thought of it that way. "It honestly was a decent car when I got it. It ran all right and took me from Twin Falls to Boise and back easily."

"What kind of cars do *they* have?" he inquires next, something in his eyes like he is trying to sort out what he is hearing.

"Brand-new Fords. My dad has a massive silver pick up with a six-foot bed and a camper. My mom has a silver SUV. They bought my sister, the one I grew up with, a new red Pontiac when she went to college." I stop there, retracing my words. *Wait. They have... And I have...*

Jasper scratches his head in thought. "Did your parents love you?"

I frown. Not that I am disappointed or anything. The car just shows what I am to my parents. "I don't want to talk about it." I proceed in the direction of my home, northwest, and I feel a tear roll down my cheek.

"Wait," Jasper replies in guilty panic, slipping back in at my side. "I didn't mean to offend you. I… Oh… Um…"

I swipe the tear away. "Don't worry about it."

"Well how about we stop at the mechanic shop. We sell cars, too. Nice cars. I can get you a discount. They are in the back out in a dirt field."

I stop once more. The chip reader I slid my new bank card through comes to mind, as does – once again – the fact that those women last night were surprised to see someone come into this small town. With that I turn to Jasper.

Jasper's hands go up, fear all over his face. "Hey. Sorry. We can do it another time."

"How are their cars here?" I ask.

"Huh?" Jaspers hands come down, and now he is confused.

"And chip readers and a hotel?"

More confusion.

"Modern clothes, shoes, purses." I look at my dress bag, not understanding how I could have missed time moving despite everything. "I bet the hotel never has a guest, yet it stays running. Athanasius even has loads of antiques and books for sale."

"Um… Where is this…" A light flicks on behind those dark eyes as I redirect, and a breeze moves that black hair into Jasper's face. "Oh! You are referring to the lockdown."

I gesture around the town and at the shops, arms full so it is awkward. "How is this place keeping up?"

"Magic, of course," Jasper responds matter-of-factly.

Now *I* am confused. "Magic locked this place, though."

Jasper chuckles. I am glad someone finds this amusing. "The lockdown spell was intricate, Robyn. It had to be to keep us and everyone in the world safe and moving with the flow of time. In fact, once complete, the magic held a constant motion through the surrounding area and states." He waves about, indicating Mountain Home, Boise, Twin Falls, and beyond. "Plus, there were magic couriers involved, so every time a local made an online order it was redirected to our specialized delivery service. Any print catalogues that existed were created and marketed here."

"Huh," I say, only from there another thought

comes to mind. "And the Stars Hollow road sign?" If this place was supposed to be *invisible* before my arrival, the sign kind of contradicted that… No, it really contradicted that. Then I point toward the freeway even though it cannot be seen.

The oncoming second chuckle Jasper clearly desires to express is smothered by a twerk of a smile. "The sign remained to keep us grounded in this world. Without it, the lockdown spell would have literally erased Stars Hollow and all its inhabitants, sending us into the universe as if we never existed. It may have even erased all magic in the world, including parlor tricks and magicians. Books. It was a powerful spell that most witches and wizards try to avoid."

My mouth opens for a comment. Jasper is indicating there are more towns like this one.

Except Jasper holds up a hand for silence, his face telling me he already knows what question is coming next. "Before you ask, the spell cast on this place wasn't like the ones currently on the other magical communities. The other lockdowns were implemented upon town founding and only required small sacrifices and grounding. There was no rush or threat or fear involved. No need to fix anything. In fact, the other communities are free to travel in and out, although no humans live there or visit. *Our* lockdown came late and required us to erase the memories of all those on earth, lock us down completely, force a utopia, and sacrifice a willing Light Witch."

"But why was the sign visible?" I interject. "I have pointed it out to my parents many times as a child."

Jasper crosses his arms and shifts his weight, then he stares off into the distance. He looks contemplative. "Did both your parents see it?" he asks.

That is an odd question, but it gets me thinking, nonetheless. My mother never replied when I asked about the sign, like she never heard me. My father, however, always told me this place was a ghost town. Did only my father see the sign and not my mother? It would make sense, my father being a true Salem descendent and not my mother.

"You are magical, Robyn," Jasper resumes.

I notice he is looking at me again. He must have figured out my train of thought.

"Magical beings and humans are not the same, so spells work different on us. While all humans were forced to turn a blind eye and forget everything about magic and this town, the magical outside this town were forced to pretend they had no clue despite knowledge of our involvement with the second witch hunt. Over time, even the magical world started to believe we no longer existed."

I absorb all the information. It makes sense, I guess. "All right," I nod.

"Soooo," Jasper draws out like he did earlier, although with caution in every bit of his expression, and he holds out both hands like a human scale. "Car or no car."

I get ready to say yes, but then I realize I probably won't use a car. Where would I go? But it would be nice to get around faster.

"So, no car?" Jasper presses.

"A bike?" I ask.

Jasper looks confused all over again. "A bike? What is a bike?"

My brows furrow. Stars Hollow has cars but no bikes?

Jasper laughs and slaps my shoulder. "Just messing with you. "We sell bikes, too."

Wands Upon a Time

A mechanic shop, hardware shop, car shop, and bike shop all in one. Who knew?

Stonewall Manor

Jasper pulls up to Stonewall Manor, named due to the fact it is no simple Victorian. Although I don't think even manor works as the place is more along the lines of castle. It is 5:20pm. I had failed to obtain a timeframe, but luckily this is a small town and everyone knows the Stonewalls eat dinner at 5:30pm. Cars already line the driveway.

"Shall I walk you to the door?" Jasper asks as he moves to shut off the key, but he stops and lets his fingers graze the chain as he gives me a questioning look.

I direct toward the double doors of the only

manor I have seen so far in this small town. It looks just as historic as everything else around here, and the porch light is on despite it being daylight and waiting for me to humiliate myself on the steps. Yes, I tripped on my own steps at Salem House when my wedges caught on the hem of my dress. I figure if I lift my skirt enough next time, it won't happen again. "No." I open the door and step out. "It is probably best if I show up alone, that way they don't think I invited a guest and I have to explain myself."

Jasper nods. I catch it just in time as I peek back inside. His pale glow is strange in the shadow of the car's interior, as are his eyes. He almost looks...

I mentally shake my head, getting that idea out.

"You are most likely right," Jasper responds, "and they don't like me anyway."

"They don't?" *That is shocking. Who wouldn't like Jasper? He is sweet, helpful, charming...* I pause in my mental list, not sure where it is going with the word *charming.*

"I will tell you later. Text me when you are ready to go." He holds up his smartphone. "I put my number into your phone while you were busy getting ready."

"Will do. Thanks." And I close the door and lift my skirt ahead of time. I picked low heeled wedges for better walking, so only the skirt is an issue.

Jasper doesn't leave right away. I know because his car engine is idling, and it continues to idle as I take the porch steps cautiously one at a time. His car wheels only begin to move as I glide up to the door and take the large knocker in hand.

The sound of the black metal device is something I have never actually heard in person before, and I am not sure I like it or not.

The door opens, and a woman in her early fifties (at least) appears. She is blond, like Leo, and her figure is that of a model in her red and silver evening gown with black feathers flowing down the skirt. Her hair is in a curly bun. She has to be six feet tall. "Robyn, my dear," she sings, though she doesn't smile. She waves me in. "Come in. Everyone is already here."

The door closes behind us, and in the quiet that follows the space of the entryway and the unknown ahead that graces my sight, I hear the mumbling of voices.

"Just this way," Samantha resumes, guiding me

further inside. I remember that is what Athanasius called her this morning. She is the mayor of Stars Hollow.

Here I notice the entryway takes up a good chunk of the front of the house and is fairly wide open. Two grand staircases curve up to the next level and are draped with red carpeting. This level, however, kind of resembles a museum with podiums and art and statues. Some paintings of the family. The setup makes our footfalls echo.

Then at last the place narrows off naturally as we pass under the staircases, alcoves of suits of armor appearing, and we make our way past a dining room. A peek shows a massive table set up with fancy dishes. The kitchen is opposite.

Now this is a strange layout.

The next room, straight at the end, is a living space of some sort. I can make out another eating area just around a stretch of wall to the right.

All goes silent and twelve individuals turn our way. I only recognize three – Sookie, Sam, and Leo. Sookie and Sam are the only ones, other than myself I am sure, who don't look like they belong here or should be dressed in such finery. From what I hear, the two

Kitchen Witches live above their diner.

"Everyone," Samantha continues to sing. It is here she slips an arm around me and grips both my shoulders.

I don't like her touching me at all, but I force back a squirm. That squirm that would wiggle me out from her grasp.

"This is Robyn Salem."

Everyone swarms forward with hellos that hit all sorts of decibels, and my blood pressure goes through the roof. Face after face from there passes my view in less than a second each, names going with them I am not sure I will remember, and everyone shakes my hand hard and violent. Even the elderly get a strong go at me.

Then questions start flying at once, and my attention swivels from one face to the next. Expressions pass like thunderous waves.

"Dinner is ready," interrupts a shaky voice. It shushes the room.

Samantha turns, and I go with her. It makes me momentarily grateful because I am not sure how much further I can restrain myself from running off. With that I spot the man who spoke – a butler, and he has to be over a hundred. Every inch of the servant tremors on thin limbs.

Samantha regains control of the room. "We shall get to know Robyn over dinner."

The shuffling of feet, some heeled and some flat. But I remain at the front with Samantha where I can feel the breaths on my back and hear the low whispers. I have a feeling dinner is going to be far more uncomfortable than anything I have ever experienced.

~*~

"Where are you from?" a female Cottonwood witch with deep brown hair and faux leaves begins as she digs into the salad in front of her. She is sitting across from me. She looks around my age, and I am thinking the name Iris.

Or maybe Iris is the girl next to her and the one speaking is Rose. I did pick up on the fact that the Cottonwoods have nature names, which goes with the fact they are Earth Witches.

I prepare to answer, except then…

"Did you go to college?" asks a male witch.

The question leaves my mouth hanging open. I am guessing this guy is also a Cottonwood. He looks to be Iris' and Rose's father. So, Alder? Or is it Rowan? I know Thorn is the son. Then there is Nepta and Jasmine, grandmother and mother.

"What do you do for a living?" someone gets in.

I snap my attention to the right, but I don't catch who spoke as they come from the other end of the table entirely, but the person sounds elderly. Male as well. Based on the direction, though, I am guessing Carlyle Stonewall, the grandfather.

"What do you plan to do now that you are here in Stars Hollow?" Possibly two or three people say at once. The two girls out of the three giggles. The male doesn't react outside of expectant eyes.

"Are you enjoying the town?"

"Have you figured out any spells or charms yet?"

Oh boy, I manage to think. Except all I can do is glance from face to face as the questions come and wait for them to stop. My brain is working to retain all the questions while trying to recall names. Only everyone seems to be blurring in thunderous waves once more. I do notice, however, that not just the founding families are here. Other families are present as well, and their names I don't know at all.

"Did you bring the grimoire?" This woman I know is Endora Stonewall. I made sure to store her name, voice, and face well the moment we all sat down. "We can cast the reading spell on you tonight."

What is this? An interview? A test? I feel like I am in one or the other, and for a position where I will be the main attraction. Like at a circus. Only I may be failing horribly. I know Serina saw me coming, but it didn't sound prophetic of anything hugely important. My gosh.

Then at last the questions cease. I know because I wait several long seconds just to make sure. So it is definitely my turn now, and it leaves my heart beating very noticeably... at least to me.

I give them all what they want. It is, after all, polite. "I am from Twin Falls," I answer, playing with my salad because talking and listening gives me no time to eat. "I have a Master of Arts in Creative Writing. I am an author."

"Oos and ahhs."

"What kind of books do you write?" Sookie asks from my right. She and her father have been silent this entire time.

I spear a tomato and watch it squirt over the leaves. "Medieval fantasy." My next words I regret before I say them. "I like to write about magic."

Everyone chuckles and laughs. Of course they do. I write about magic and they are all witches. *I* am a witch.

"There are elves in my stories, and dwarves and fairies and such, so the magic is different," I add, looking around at everyone again. They all find it easy to listen and talk and eat at once.

And laugh. They still laugh.

I blush and force the tomato off my fork. "I used to be a substitute teacher, too, though. Not sure if there is a need for that here, but…"

"There may be," Samantha's husband chimes in from the left head of the table. I can see him quite well as I am close to him. His name is Darren. "We have only one school, but when teachers or assistants are sick the principle takes over, so she may be glad to have you around."

I nod, not adding that I also used to be a realtor because, well, I don't want to.

That is when a tune goes off. It is short, but

persistent.

"Forgive me," Samantha apologizes from the right head of the table.

I lean discreetly forward just in time to catch Samantha pull out a phone from somewhere under the table and take a peek, and in the new quiet I take a bite of my salad.

"Sheriff Wolfe?" Darren asks.

Samantha nods.

"Did he catch Jasper?" their daughter, Tabatha, asks. She looks about eighteen.

The tomato I still have on my fork because it refused to come off earlier goes down whole and I choke as I do what I am assuming is supposed to be a gasp of horror.

Sookie pats me on the back and hands me my water.

I take it with teary eyes and drink heavily, my ears wide open for answers. Not sure if any will come, though, as I am positive that kind of information is private.

"Yes," comes the answer to my surprise. "Caught him about fifteen minutes ago. Sheriff Wolfe just finished booking him. He put up quite a fight. I just can't believe, in such a small town like this, it took so long to find him. Three hours."

"Why?" I blurt, my voice hoarse. And three hours does sound like a long time, but he had been with me so they might not have thought about that.

Sookie keeps patting my back.

"We think his demon half went crazy," Darren responds.

I am not sure if I am still choking or not breathing, so I take another drink.

"He is only half human, so with the lockdown spell broken he may not have control or is finally allowed to let loose. He sucked a human's energy clean out of him and left him dead outside The Haunted Inn."

He's an energy vampire? I process mentally. I am not horrified by that or insulted he didn't tell me. Just surprised. I had been correct from the start. He is a vampire, although not the blood drinking kind.

"Dear me," Granny Endora Stonewall chirps up. "Robyn looks a bit pale."

"Probably because she was with him today," Sam answers from Sookie's other side. "They had lunch at my diner."

"Most likely she also didn't know he is half energy vampire," Leo adds as confirmation, and rather stiffly and arrogantly. "He is quite secretive about it. Most likely even attempted to use her as an alibi. Disgusting."

Alibi? The room spins and it is hard not to gasp and fall out of my seat.

"Sheriff Wolfe did text that Jasper claimed he was with Robyn today," Samantha resumes. "All day. He had an entire story ready. Except when Sheriff Wolfe called Sara at Bejeweled, the woman stated neither Jasper nor Robyn entered the shop today. He couldn't get Jasper's father on the line to confirm anything further, but a few witnesses stated Jasper and Robyn parted ways after lunch. Witnesses in the diner said that at one point Jasper left the table for about ten minutes, enough time to go out a window and commit the crime."

I begin shaking my head, and once more I become center of attention. Samantha has been talking as if I am not right here listening. Everyone around me has even forgotten about me, something I am regrettably used to. Now I have their attention, though. "Jasper doesn't lie. He was with me all day. Never left my sight." My voice doesn't sound like my own, neither does my body feel like my own. "We had lunch together, he took me dress shopping and bike shopping, we went for a walk in the park so I could see the gazebo, and then he dropped me off here. The only time he used the restroom was at my house around 3:00."

Silence. Everyone exchanges glances.

"What time was the murder at?" someone I forgot the name of asks.

"Sheriff Wolfe puts it at 12:30 this afternoon," Samantha states, sitting regally. She reaches for her glass and takes a sip.

Now I know it was noon when we ate, but I have no idea the exact time. Maybe Jasper *did* use me as an alibi.

"No," Sam interjects.

I lean over my salad again, discreetly, just as the butler comes through and takes it. I didn't even see him come in.

"Jasper couldn't have done it, then. He and Robyn sat down in my diner at 12:15 and then helped put out a fire at exactly 12:30."

That makes me wonder where Sam was when the questioning was going on today. Why was only Bejeweled and some random people questioned? Why wasn't *I* called?

Maybe the police got what they needed and figured they had no reason to talk to Sam, my inner voice suggests. *And no one has your phone number yet, except Jasper and Athanasius.*

"If Robyn truly says Jasper never left her sight until 3:00, Jasper is in the clear."

More silence, in which time Samantha pulls her phone back out. "Give me a moment." She starts dialing. This isn't a text conversation.

The blinging of the screen buttons, though, makes me anxious and I grip my stomach. I think I might have a headache, too. My friend is in jail for a murder he didn't commit, and for a split second I actually thought he did it. And now I feel guilty for being surprised by Jasper's demon half in any way, shape, or form. I am part demon, part human, part witch. I am a Light and Dark Witch, although thinking about it now it doesn't make sense how I can be both light and dark.

A squeaky hello draws me back to the moment.

More squeaks follow.

"Yes," Samantha responds. "I am afraid there is a problem, Sheriff Wolfe. I fear we made a mistake. Jasper's alibi holds up. I have Robyn, Sam, and Sookie here who can back it up."

More squeaks I unfortunately can't sort out, and they don't sound happy.

Samantha nods and *mhms*. "Yes, I know about the pocket watch, the witnesses, and the breaking of the lockdown spell. But maybe it is possible the boy lost the watch outside the inn and everything else is just coincidences and lies. Maybe even misunderstandings."

"He took me to the inn," I say desperately, sinking further over the table. "Last night." I hope that helps.

"Robyn says he was there last night," she translates over. "With her." More *mhms*. "All right. Thank you, Sheriff Wolfe." She hangs up.

I hold what breath I can.

"He is being released," Samantha announces.

I sag, and there I find Sookie's hand still on my back. I want to text Jasper to come get me, but the main course is only now being set down.

Equality

The evening is strangely cool for June, and I find I am in want of a shawl when I cross my arms and lean sideways into the railing of the Stonewall Manor porch. My eyes are on the driveway, where everyone is gathered and getting out their last-minute chatter.

"It has been five minutes," Leo speaks as he comes up the steps, walks around me, and braces himself against the railing looking out. "Has Jasper responded yet? Is he on his way?"

I sigh and look down at my phone. I click the side button to flash the screen on, but no message icon appears. Just the big numbers telling me it is 7:35.

"I could drive you."

I glance over at Leo. It is eerie how this guy goes from snobbish, to arrogant, to nice. Then a breeze that sends my hair dancing slightly and I get an uncomfortable sensation, one that tells me not to get in any car with this guy. "No. That is all right. I will wait." But it is not just uncomfortableness, I want to see Jasper. I need to make sure Jasper is all right. I can't end today without seeing him.

Leo speaks nothing more. He simply waits with me, eyes out at the guests. Cars are beginning to pull out now.

"You should consider the offer, dear," Samantha speaks up as she makes her way from a newly parting group and joins us. "It is no trouble at all."

I shake my head. "It has only been a short while. He might be showering or misplaced his phone." I hope it is one or both of those things and Jasper didn't forget or ditch me. Although forgetting is acceptable, too, after the night he had.

Ten minutes later.

All the cars are gone, the Stonewalls are gathered

Wands Upon a Time

on the porch with me, and I am shivering. It isn't less than seventy degrees, but I am shivering.

"You should take my grandson's offer," Granny Endora speaks up.

"I agree," Grandfather Carlyle chimes in.

My expression falls, eyes darting across the large driveway. It still isn't dark yet, being only 7:45 on a summer evening, so the property and all around it for as far as the eye can see is visible. This time of day always throws me off year-round.

"He isn't coming," Leo comments. "I'm sorry to say it, but that is how demons are. Vampires are the worst as…"

My brows snap together at the idea of what will be said next, and I feel a fire burn within me. It is enough to get me to direct and face the guy at my side with all intent to teach him a lesson about all living beings being equal. He should know about equality if his family promotes it, although maybe not if his family truly consists of only witches. Maybe their equality stance is just a gig. "I am part demon!" I say instead.

"You are different, Robyn. You are part witch, part human, part demon. And that demon part is so small.

Your light outshines the darkness you were born with. Your witch side outshines your human side. You are very much a Light Witch."

My brows come closer together. He is mentally eradicating all I am and making me what he desires to see. Only I know where this fight will lead, and I will lose as always. "I see there is no point getting into this," I state, cutting off my attempt to argue. Also, there is no reason to make myself sick. Anger makes me sick. "I am walking home." I push away from the railing with that.

"Now I don't think that is a good idea," Darren interrupts."

I twist to find Leo's father sitting with Endora and Carlyle in a porch swing for three. Tabatha and Samantha are leaning against the wall. I have to admit, only Samantha and Leo are unbearable, although Leo more so. The mother and son haven't done much to create my opinion of them, it is just that I can't stand the two of them. It is a vibe I get, like when you first meet someone and you just know you won't get along.

"There is a murderer out there," Darren continues softly and with much concern, "one we know is a demon, and you cannot fight him off even if you are a partial demon. Let my son drive you."

I lift my skirt and proceed down the steps. I know Darren means well, but I am *not* getting into a car with his son for any reason. Not even if a dragon is chasing me. "I will be fine. It is light out and you all taught me defensive charms for the last hour. I can handle myself." With that said, I start my way off the property without a second thought.

"Follow her, Leo," Darren resumes. "In your car. Be nice. She is feeling hurt and most likely abandoned."

I hear footsteps. They move quite quickly. Then a door opens and closes, a garage door rolls up. There is honestly no arguing about this, either. Leo is going to follow me no matter what.

In minutes, the large driveway, surrounded by gravel, flowers, grass, and those firefly lights, turns to road. I begin making my way north along the countryside, the cluster of homes on my right just visible over the very new high fences. I hope I am not getting turned around, that would be embarrassing. It shouldn't be that hard to find my way from the lower west to upper west side of town. It shouldn't be hard to find my way through a small town, period.

Then Leo's Lamborghini (only the heavens knows why he has this car in a small town that has been in lockdown) pulls up alongside me. There he rolls down the window with a click of a button. I bet he doesn't even know how to use the old-style window roller. Finally he grins broad and shows all his teeth. "Just let me know if you change your mind. This car can go from zero to sixty faster than you can blink. He pats the window frame here. "This baby will make you feel like a goddess."

I make a face. I just can't help it. How can anyone find that kind of a line alluring?

There is a shrug from just beyond my peripheral, and Leo reaches over and turns on his radio. Music begins blaring, and it shakes the frame of the car and the few trees and bushes around us. I think it even moves a tumbleweed a few inches.

Now I have to listen to music meant to make him sound tough and cool in his tough and cool Lamborghini.

~*~

Salem House turns out to be further than expected on foot. This town is bigger than first perceived, in fact. Or maybe it is walking in wedges that are basically heels, and in a dress I have to keep holding up to prevent myself from tripping.

Which is what I do. I trip. Except this time because I step wrong, causing me to land on my hands and knees and scrape them along the pavement as I slide slightly. I feel sticky blood run along my palms and between my skin and dress fast. I think I taste it, too.

I try to stand, but my foot gets caught on my dress. I hear a tear and I collapse all over again. I should have seen that coming.

The Lamborghini door opens but doesn't close, and I turn over onto my rear just as Leo crouches down. He shakes his head. "Women," he grunts, then he pulls out his wand, a dark, crooked thing, and speaks a single word. "Reparea."

My dress stitches right up, covering my knee that had been exposed, and sparkles like new.

"You all get upset over nothing, overreact, and can't accept a man's help. When will you all learn?" He stands back up. "Now, get in the car."

My face scrunches up in further disgust of this man. I can't believe he thinks he can speak to me like this, while I am down on the ground and vulnerable. No, I won't have this. Not again. "No!"

"No?" His features stare down at me funny, but then he shoots his wand out again and gives the spot on my dress a wave. A new word spills from his lips. "Lacrimea."

The tear opens back up.

I look down at the place where my knee once more pokes out in horror. I knew I hated this guy. My gut is never wrong.

"Then I guess you don't need help with that, either. By the way…" He looks proud of himself here, like he is about to get his way after all, "doing it yourself is personal gain. Which means consequences."

A squeal of tires. Both our attentions snap around just as a car zooms our way from the direction of my house. It takes maybe five seconds after that and the vehicle swerves and skids to a stop, leaving a trail of black in the road that will be there forever.

It is Jasper.

My friend shoves his door open, slides out, and slams it shut. The sound echoes around us, sending birds flying out of nearby trees, and his sweet face looks so menacing and terrifying it has *me* scared. "I saw that!" he hollers with pure defensive anger. "You sicko!"

"Me?" Leo gestures to himself, astonishment all over his face. But anyone around will know something is about to go down because that isn't just any face of astonishment. Then he smirks, scoffing a little. "You are calling *me* a sicko?" His features change again. I didn't know a single face could have so many different expressions at once or in a row, and this time it is rage. "You demonic half-breed piece of shit!" he growls out, sending a strange smokey appearance across his blue irises that turns them grey. "Know your place!"

They storm toward each other. Unbelievably, Leo actually steps over me in doing so.

I attempt to scramble to my feet and stop the fight that no doubt is coming, but I get caught on my dress again and fall back down.

"You may have everyone else in this town fooled into believing you are a saint," Jasper retaliates in his own rage, getting face to face with Leo with no hesitation, "but I know you are as dark as they come!"

Leo laughs. His wand is still in his hand, and I see it twitching.

"Just admit it! You are no longer a Weather Witch! You sold your soul to the darkness!"

I finally push up to the sound of Leo laughing some more, much louder than before. "Stoooop iiiit!" I scream… no, screech. The words take my entire body to let out, every muscle in my face to form, and with them panic rises through every fiber of my being. I can recall all the fights I have seen on television shows and in movies, none of which end well. And I have a horrible feeling this one won't go well for Jasper.

That triggers the migraine, and tears of pain pour down my cheeks, over my jaw, and along my neck. I grab my head, the pulsing starting in my temples. "Stop it!" I weakly repeat as forcefully as I can, only it makes my head hurt more, and suddenly I can feel my heart beating desperately.

It is unnaturally hot now.

Leo points backward to his car without looking at me, his wand going up to Jasper. It is aimed directly at my friend's chest. "Get in the car, Robyn!"

Jasper shoves Leo, sending him stumbling. "How dare you speak to her like that!"

Leo shoves back, thankfully forgetting his wand in the moment of hostility. "If she had just gotten in the car at the house this wouldn't have happened!"

Something comes over me then. Not sure what, but I rip open the draw string of my purse and pull out my own wand. I point it at Leo and say the body binding charm I was taught approximately an hour ago. "Ligabis!"

Leo stiffens and falls backward onto the pavement.

There is barely time to register the severity of what I did after that, the fact that I attacked the grandson of the coven leader, when arms swoop around me and pull me in close. I don't even have time to blink or suck in a breath.

"I am so sorry, Robyn," Jasper says against my ear as frantically as any being can. "I was upset and confused. I wasn't thinking straight. I turned off my phone, believing our friendship over since you know what I am, and crawled into bed for the night. I figured your statement to the police was simply doing the right thing. I have too many horrible past experiences."

I hug him back with that last comment, possibly a bit slowly. I am not used to this. It feels strange, awkward, but nice. I like hugging Jasper, and then my arms go completely around him.

"My dad had to talk sense into me," Jasper resumes. "Then I saw your text and panicked. I drove over as fast as possible. Please forgive me."

"I am not upset with you," I answer, and I bury my face as my temples remind me of my headache by expanding into the place behind my left eye for a round of fresh new tears. It hurts massively, and I know full well it will be there all night long keeping me awake.

There my stomach growls. I hadn't actually eaten dinner. The salad went before I had more than one bite and my nerves didn't allow me to eat the crab with rice and corn.

Jasper laughs and pulls away, holding me at arm's length. There he smiles his smile. "Did they not feed you enough?"

I frown and look down at our feet, flinching a little with the three new intense pounds against my temples from making that motion.

"Hey," he lifts my head gently by the chin, and my eyes that I am sure are strained and red just don't have the energy to actually make any sort of contact. "You look miserable. More so than I was hours ago. In fact, I can hear your heart racing."

I grip my head, not able to fight it any longer. "I didn't eat at all," I say, like that is the excuse for my current state. "I answered a bunch of questions and then I was worried about you. After that it was basic wand lessons for protection."

"Well come along. I will get you home." His hand slips along my back, but then stops. "I forgot about Leo."

We both look at the bulked-up witch on the ground. I took down Thor, and that amuses me for a moment until I remember he is Leo Stonewall.

"I think unbind him once we are safe in the car," Jasper suggests."

I shake my head, regretting it only after the action, and imagine Leo using magic as revenge as we drive away. "The charm will fade after ten minutes. It is designed to hold until a physical means is obtained to restrain him or for the victim to get away."

Jasper nudges me forward, "Then let us hope no one finds him before that. Let's get going. We can call Athanasius and he will help with the protection of the house. I won't leave you alone until I know you are safe from Leo and whatever vampire is out there."

Wands Upon a Time

"I think I am more worried about the Stonewalls," I respond, letting Jasper take me to the passenger side and open the door for me. He helps me sit. "Leo could say I attacked him for no reason, or you attacked him, or we ganged up on him, or…" I am sure there are many things he could say, but my head hurts too much.

"Naw," Jasper waves my fears off. "Fret not. Leo would have to explain why he got out of his precious car to begin with. He would have to explain your torn and dirty dress. Plus, there is such a thing as a truth serum, which Endora isn't afraid to use to find out who tells the truth and who lies."

I relax, but only enough to let my head fall back and my eyes to close.

For Good of All

A hand on my shoulder shakes me lightly. I moan, shift my head painfully to the left, and pry my reluctant eyes open. Jasper smiles at me, his hair a wild black mass more so than usual, and I remember we are in his car.

I rub my eyes and blink, catching sight of Athanasius in the last stretch of sunlight just beyond my friend. It seems a bit later than it had been when I closed my eyes, though still some time away from night.

"I called him," Jasper explains, "I let you sleep until he got here. Your heart was racing so fast and you were beginning to burn up. I figured some rest might help."

"Ready to go inside?" Athanasius asks. "I brought some extra items that I figured you wouldn't have as Serina didn't use them." Here he lifts a small bag, which clanks and jingles a bit.

I don't say anything, I just reach for the door and press on the handle. My palms hurt as I do so, though. They are scraped up enough that using any sort of pressure reminds me of what happened. Stepping out I see the knee that pokes out is just as bad as my hands.

My feet touch the ground at last, and I recall why I like flats over wedges and heels. I think I have blisters forming already from trying to walk home in these things.

Jasper appears in front of me. "Need help?" And his hand shoots out to me.

I nod, slipping my arm into his grasp, and let him pull me out.

"I think it is safe to take off your shoes," Jasper comments. "We are on the driveway and the sidewalk leads from here straight to the house."

That isn't a bad idea, so I bend down as Jasper braces me and slip each wedge off with a finger. The cool driveway on my bare feet feels better, although I make sure to walk on my toes anyway. From there we venture to my front door, where I can now hear Missy yipping.

Missy yips more often than barks.

"Keys?" Athanasius asks, palm going out for them. "I can unlock the door for you."

I hold out my little purse, my shoes dangling next to them. I am still in possession of my wand, I notice. Somehow my wand goes unseen to this point.

Athanasius takes my purse and pulls out my keys. They are in the lock in seconds, and Missy bounds out like a bunny, getting under everyone's feet as we make our way inside. We all head for the living room.

But something is different.

"Where did that television come from?" Jasper reacts.

Those are my exact thoughts, but mine more dramatic as my attention lands on the flat screen television built into the wall above the fireplace. The mantel holds a movie player (I say movie player because it takes VHS and DVD); a VHS rewinder is next to it. Surrounding all that, and the fireplace, is a brand-new nook with all my tapes and discs. I can tell right away everything is organized by category and device.

"The house," Athanasius replies. "It is giving Robyn everything she needs. The refrigerator and pantry are most likely stocked as well."

I remember my books in the attic as Jasper and I sit on the couch, Missy making her way between us happily, and Athanasius sets his bag and my purse on the center table. "Can the house magic over what is already mine?" I ask, curious about that now. I had been more stunned that morning than anything else. "Like, stuff I had no choice but to leave behind?"

"I believe so." Athanasius opens the bag and pulls out horseshoes, small bundles of bells, and a few herbs. "Why do you ask?"

I look out the open doorway, but of course I can't see the stairs from here. "Because all my personal books are in the attic, but I didn't bring them along." I redirect to the movies. "Those movies are mine, too. Although the television and player are new."

Athanasius takes up the seat on my other side. "Hm." He grabs a horseshoe here. "I guess the house is reading you. It is learning what you like and dislike, which involves your books and movies. Now…" he holds up the horseshoe.

"You know," Jasper interrupts. "I don't recall an attic, either." Here he picks up herbs resembling fresh green leaves and eyes them funny, like he has never seen anything like them before. In all honesty, neither have I.

"It appeared this morning," I comment, and I grab some of those leafy herbs, too, for inspection. They appear to be from some sort of small plant.

"As I was saying," Athanasius continues, holding out the horseshoe before us and waving it.

"This is catnip," Jasper interrupts again. "I am surprised Coco isn't running in here for it."

"Coco doesn't care for catnip, or anyone who isn't me."

"Ah." He sets the catnip down, but I continue to hold mine for no particular reason.

Athanasius grunts.

"Sorry," Jasper and I say at once, and we both look to the item our wizard companion directs us to.

"I brought horseshoes. Jasper here," Athanasius gestures, "can nail them above the doors and gate. From inside, that is. They must face up." With that he grabs the other two and passes them over. "I am thinking of attaching bells to them as well, and protection satchels. I figure we can't be too cautious if there is a murderer out there and Leo is as Jasper states."

It hadn't clicked before, but…

"You sold your soul to the darkness!"

I look from Jasper to Athanasius and back. "You guys think Leo is a Dark Witch," I say. Then I see those blue eyes go grey and smokey in my mind.

"Yes," Jasper states. "I have never been able to get Athanasius to believe me until now because of the lockdown spell and the fact Leo comes from a founding family. My theory is that Leo is powerful enough to have had more leeway than expected, so he turned. He just couldn't do much. Now, though…"

"There is still no proof," Athanasius comments, passing over three sets of bells to join the horseshoes. "I do believe you now, but it will be hard to prove as Leo is known for being unpleasant by some and a saint by others. He has been unpleasant since he learned to walk and talk. It is his upbringing. He is spoiled and the oldest. I am surprised his boyfriend puts up with him."

"I hear they are engaged now," Jasper adds. "And there is something about *him*, too. I don't think he is a full witch but a half-demon like me."

Athanasius shakes his head. "Proof. You need proof, Jasper."

Jasper crosses his arms and leans back. There he crosses one leg over the other. "I will find some. You will see."

"For now, though," Athanasius says, "go to the shed out back and get a hammer and some nails. I will go up to the attic for the satchel items. I also need to heal Robyn's wounds and fix her dress."

~*~

An hour later, my wounds are healed, my dress is fixed and clean, both doors and the gate have a horseshoe with bells and a satchel, and every set of blinds hides protection items. Jasper spends a good amount of this time checking all locks and latches; the attic is no exception despite the fact it can disappear. He even examines the automatic dog door, Missy on his heels with her rear wagging.

"Did we miss anything?" Jasper asks as we gather back in the living room. His question is directed to Athanasius. "Is there a spell, maybe, for the property itself?"

My brows rise at that question, one after the other, and not just at the fact a spell would be far more over the top than what has already been done. Jasper is being protective of me, beyond what happened on the road. I guess I did the same with him today, too, and that gets to me as well as I wonder if all friends do that.

"Actually," Athanasius responds, pulling out a small sheet of paper and passing it to me.

I take it and see a short little poem. That old-style calligraphy is just readable.

Sea, air, fire, earth,
guard this home, bless this hearth.
Keep this place safe and all within,
drive away all harm and fear.
For good of all, this bond begins.
By earth's elements, this spell is done.

"That is an incantation I have heard Serina use many times. You need to speak it as you touch each satchel. It will ultimately create a barrier that leads from one to the other, which in the end will surround the house. No one who intends you harm will be able to set foot in here, and all but those in this room will need to be invited inside."

Well that is nifty.

"Start with the front door and move through the house in a circle. You will have to go outside in the middle of it all to include the gate."

Another half hour is spent doing this before I finally get to eat some sandwiches the house supplied.

Team Paranormal

Hawthorne leaps onto Athanasius' desk in a flurry of white, miraculously missing stacks of books and papers. There he sits down, tail swooping around him. I can't get over how adorably cute, fluffy, and small he is for a full-grown cat.

No, not a cat. Hawthorne is a wizard... *Was* a wizard.

Then those blue eyes glare at me and slowly form into slits. Except Hawthorne dares say nothing in front of his master.

"So what exactly happened yesterday?"

Athanasius directs from our long silence as he sorts a few piles and pushes them aside, but his cleaning efforts don't make much of a difference. His space still looks like the mess of a scatterbrain, and possibly more so today. "With the arrest, I mean. All I heard was you were apprehended and charged with murder. Everyone was running about gossiping, but no one knew much else."

Jasper leans into the desk with a groan and his forehead falls into his palm. He woke up like this, and honestly so did I. We both had enough of yesterday to last a life time.

"Forgive me," Athanasius resumes, sifting through some more stuff to his right. "I should have figured it was a touchy subject. I just wanted to get you two talking and maybe help ease your minds. Talking things out can be helpful."

"It's all right," Jasper replies defeatedly, and he straightens with a deep sigh that rolls through his entire body. Except then his gaze drifts down and he ends up staring at his open palms on the desk.

I distract myself by petting Hawthorne. No one is looking anyway, and all I have to add is what I was told over dinner. Those things seem to be topics for Jasper to divulge, not me. Everything after is well known.

Hawthorne begins to purr and lean in, a paw going up.

"I am honestly still processing it all," Jasper finally offers up. "It happened so fast and no one questioned me. It was like I was guilty on the spot, no matter what I said or how much I fought. Then all witnesses lied, and for a long while I thought so did Robyn. I thought I had been set up somehow for being half demon."

That last part gets me to side-eye my friend. He hates a part of himself, and I sympathize with that. I personally don't hate myself for being a witch or demon or even human, but for another reason I do not wish to reveal quite yet.

"My mind got really messed up in there. I know I wasn't locked up long, but it was enough to break me."

Jasper reaches into his pocket here and pulls out something silver. There is a train engraved on the back of the thing and a chain attached to his belt loop. He turns it over and I see it is a pocket watch.

"I lost this on the freeway," Jasper continues. "At least I figured it was the freeway. I couldn't see how it was anywhere else. Sheriff Wolfe said Deputy Huckly found it outside The Haunted Inn, though, by the body. Magic showed only my prints." He began to fiddle with the watch. "It took a bit to convince him to let me have this back when I was released. I broke into tears and fell to my knees begging. It was my great-great-grandpa's."

And there I notice discoloration along Jasper's wrists. They peek out from under the long black sleeves I just realize he is wearing. He must be hot in that shirt, but then again... Vampire.

I reach over without thinking, and he flinches away.

I blush.

"My wrists are sensitive," Jasper explains. "Please don't take offense." He rolls up his sleeves with that, revealing not just bruises but burns. They scrape a bit further up along his wrists, too, showing how much he fought against whatever held him.

"I don't understand," I direct. "Why didn't you have Athanasius heal those last night? He healed me and fixed my dress."

"Because the cuffs used on him," Athanasius explains, still working his way through the catastrophe that is his desk, "are designed with a curse type of magic to restrain vampires. And witches and wizards cannot heal demons. They will be there for a while."

"I think smoke actually came off my skin," Jasper adds painfully as he stuffs his watch back in his pocket. "Every now and then it feels like the cuffs are still on me." He rubs his wrists here, and sadness fills his eyes. A tear escapes.

"They judged you quick," Athanasius responds, "and all based on being half demon. It is not fair. Sheriff Wolfe grew up with you. He should know you better than that. And this town should know better than that."

"Sheriff Wolfe…" Jasper retaliates. Yes, he is getting defensive. "… like every other magical person in this town, hates me."

"I don't," Athanasius replies. "Neither do the Thymes or Robyn. In fact, I am sure you are wrong about Sheriff Wolfe. I heard the sheriff wasn't even pleased to arrest you. And if you think about it, he gave you back your watch rather than make an excuse to hold onto it."

I stop petting Hawthorne and take Jasper by the shoulder. This is not something I normally do, but I have seen it done in a movie once and I want him to know I care. There I give him a smile, which he half returns without looking my way. "He is right," I say. "I like you a lot. You are kind and sweet and helpful. You are my best friend, and that is saying something coming from me because I am picky. And you know what?"

"What?" Jasper asks, spying my way a bit.

"You are the only one I let hug me."

"I like you, too," Hawthorne jumps in, "even if you *are* a scrawny thing that refuses to pet me. I call you my best friend, too."

"Thank you," Jasper says with one more escaped tear. "I needed to hear that. I shook off these feelings yesterday evening, but it all rushed back over me when I got into bed. My hatred of my demon half came back. So thank you again."

"I am guessing there are no clues as to who the real murderer is?" I ask next, looking from Jasper to Athanasius to get this subject redirected. Only from there a horrible idea hits. "Is it possible this could come back to Jasper? They said his pocket watch was evidence."

They both shrug, but it is the wizard who responds. "I haven't heard anything about that so far, and I doubt anyone will come for Jasper with your testimony.

Even the Thymes will stand with Jasper, as will I."

"How many energy vampires live here? How many demons?" I inquire further, hoping to get some sort of scope on the population and how easy it would be to sort out the identity of the true murderer. If the police can get it wrong so fast from the get-go, I don't see any hope in them figuring out anything later without some help.

"Not many," Jasper answers, rubbing his wrists again as he makes an unpleasant face.

That sounds reassuring.

"I am the only half-demon. That this town knows of, that is." He is referring to Leo's fiancé. "There are twenty-two full ones out there with only two families of vampires. None drink blood as those are forbidden above ground to prevent blood-borne diseases."

I think about that, and from there wonder how the only two vampire families connect to Jasper. I also think about how it doesn't seem logical that Jasper lost his pocket watch at the inn, yet it was found there by the body of a human who had their energy sucked clean out of them. Unless the watch was planted, but that would mean someone was out on the freeway with us. Or Jasper lost the watch earlier in the day and hadn't noticed until he got home.

"Well whoever it is," Athanasius jumps back in, "has Sheriff Wolfe considering a curfew. I overheard him, Deputy Huckly, and Samantha Stonewall in the diner this morning talking about making it mandatory for all citizens to be home with their doors and windows locked before the sun sets. They are even thinking of asking everyone to only go out if necessary and to make sure it is in groups. This may be a small town, but a lot can happen in the shadows."

The front bell chimes.

"Hello?" a familiar female voice calls out, yet for some reason I cannot place it.

I twist despite all the clutter blocking the view.

"Alyssa!" Jasper hisses. "Make sure nothing magical is out."

I double check my fanny pack, which holds my two satchels, as I scan the desk. I pat my back pocket to verify my wand is hidden away. I have no recollection of bringing anything else.

"Hello?" Alyssa calls out again.

"Over here!" Athanasius calls back.

"My," Alyssa continues all singsong. "I have

never been in here. I bet you have ghosts hidden away all over the place. I should bring my EMF reader some time, if that is all right with you."

I exchange a look with Jasper. Alyssa had an EMF reader when I first met her, and she looked silly using it.

"Have you ever had books or things just go flying or fall over?" Alyssa continues.

"Not that I am aware of," Athanasius responds, "but I see no reason for you not to be able to investigate."

Alyssa finally appears. She made her way through quite well for a first timer.

"How many times do I have to tell you," Jasper finally gets in, "there are…"

"No such thing as ghosts," Alyssa finishes, and she begins fishing in a bulky bag hanging at her side. "Yeah, yeah, yeah. Explain that to my video." And she steps out of the row straight across from the desk.

"Video?" I blink. "You have a video of a ghost?" Excitement gets me with that thought. I should tell you, I tried ghost hunting once in a cemetery with a tape recorder, but I got nothing. "Cool! I want to see!" I almost leap away from the desk then, but I restrain myself and wait.

Alyssa smirks. "Well, not a ghost, but..." she pulls out a video camera, an actual video camera, and opens up the screen. A press of a button sends a ding echoing in the air. "I think you and Jasper will find this fascinating." Only with that she stops and looks over her device at Athanasius. "Maybe you, too, if you are what I think you are."

I suddenly have a bad feeling and I no longer want to see this video, but at the same time I do.

"Here," Alyssa proceeds as she steps closer and holds out her video camera where all three of us can hover over it. She reaches forward and clicks play.

A wide country road appears on the small screen. Music is blaring in the background and I can see that dang Lamborghini with Leo behind the wheel. Camera me is clearly trying to ignore the man despite him being obnoxiously right there going about five miles per hour.

"Looks like Leo Stonewall and the new Salem girl," camera Alyssa whispers. "Rylee? Roxie? Something like that. Do you all remember me saying I think the Stonewalls are witches, well I think this girl here is a descendent of Serina Salem who died back in

1889. I still believe that woman's mysterious death at twenty-five was a sacrifice. There hasn't been a Salem in Stars Hollow in over a hundred years. In fact, not a soul has come or gone from this place. *I have tried to leave, but for some reason I always find myself driving back home."*

The camera jiggles a bit and goes down. A short row of trees blur by, tumbleweeds blur by. I think I see a fence and a cow. Then grass appears. There isn't really much, though, to hide Alyssa or the camera in daylight, and at this point I am surprised I didn't see her out there. Or Leo didn't see her. Why didn't Jasper see her?

At last camera me trips. There is a slight struggle that results in me staying on the ground. What isn't seen is my dress tearing. That is when camera Leo opens his door and gets out, he bends before camera me.

Oh my gosh! My eyes go wide and my mouth partially falls open. I am not sure that expresses enough of my horror, however.

The next moments flash forward in my mind with Leo's words just mumbles because Alyssa is still too far away to catch voices. Somehow I glance up, though, to find my expression mirrored on Jasper's face.

Athanasius' is just as bad and he wasn't even there.

A look back down and I catch the moment camera Alyssa dares to move even closer, grass rustling under her with each breath she works to restrain. Camera me and camera Leo bounce in and out of view.

"I think I just heard a spell," camera Alyssa speaks up, her struggle to crawl notable.

"Now, get in the car," comes Leo's words at last, and they sound arrogant even on camera.

Camera Alyssa halts and focuses in again.

I have to say, camera Leo isn't terrifying. He is more terrifying in person when he hovers over me all demanding. Just like my father used to do.

"No!" I hear camera me say furiously from the ground.

"No?"

Hearing that response now, I note I truly baffled the Thor wannabe. Only that realization doesn't prevent my new desire to shake my head in horror as I watch camera Leo point his wand at me for a second time, but the action fails to come.

"Lacrimea."

"There, hear that?" camera Alyssa comments

further. "I wonder what it means. What did he do?"

"Then I guess you don't need help with that, either," camera Leo resumes. "By the way…" I can't quite make out facial expressions, but I can fill all that in from memory. "… doing it yourself is personal gain. Which means consequences."

Jasper's car squeals onto the screen. I think my heart stops and I fight with myself to look away, but I can't. I can't even pinch myself to verify if this is a dream or not. This has to be a dream. A nightmare.

"I saw that!" enters Jasper. "You sicko!"

I think I blackout for a moment. I am not sure.

"You demonic half-breed piece of shit! Know your place!"

Again I think I blackout, until…

"Stoooop iiiit!" camera me screeches. It sounds so strange on camera.

The shoving commences.

And…

"Ligabis!"

Leo drops like a brick.

Alyssa presses pause and closes her video camera.

Wands Upon a Time

"We were acting," Jasper offers up clearly without thought, and he hides it poorly, too. His attempt at a defiant posture doesn't even do any good.

Alyssa motions to reopen the camera, satisfaction gleaming off her like the sun. "Should I show you the next ten minutes?"

Movement from behind the desk.

Alyssa jumps back, drawing me away from that movement, and her skin goes ashen to the point her freckles even vanish. "Hey." Her fear shows in her tone, but also the threat behind it, too. "I have these saved everywhere. Someone will come across my files and they will be revealed to the world. You can't hide forever."

It takes much effort, an eternity, but I follow her gaze and discover Athanasius with a crooked wooden staff in hand. There is a swirling blue-white stone tucked away at the top.

"Trust me," Athanasius speaks with much authority, that stone at the top lighting up. "There will be no evidence. After I erase your memory, all your records will vanish. Even if you sent them to friends, they will vanish."

Alyssa snaps her gaze desperately to me, then Jasper.

Athanasius' staff goes up, the light of the stone brightening to a pure white, and something occurs to me. Two somethings. Maybe Alyssa knowing about us isn't all bad.

"Wait!" My hand shoots out between Athanasius and Alyssa. Pretty stupid, I know. What would that do?

The light snuffs out.

"Robyn," Athanasius breathes, his staff back at his side. He gives me a look of sympathy. "We must. It is for everyone's protection."

"He is right," Jasper agrees wearily as he gives out against the desk again and resumes rubbing his wrists. "If her video gets out, it could mean a third witch hunt. Humans and witches and shifters and demons will die left and right. We may not be able to get out of it this time."

That is absolutely a reasonable concern, yet I shake my head as Alyssa backs away. The red head's terror is clear even in my peripheral because it makes her eyes two giant white and emerald orbs. There is no chance of escape, however, as this shop is a maze of hoarded antiques and books. In her desperation, she will fumble and get lost. With that I point at the video camera still in Alyssa's grasp. "She has video of Leo attacking me." I look to Jasper. "Of attacking you. Of being racist."

Something in Jasper perks up.

"We can't just let that information disappear forever, and if we can gather more like it – proof that Leo is a Dark Witch – we have him cornered. Right now, that is mere proof he is a jerk and a racist, but eventually he will mess up big time. We can bring him down to where he had me last night."

"That is a brilliant idea!" Jasper grins from ear to ear.

"No," Athanasius responds, holding his ground. His short stature doesn't work against him. "She has proof of magic. It is too dangerous. Exposing Leo isn't worth this." His staff goes back up and that stone once more begins to glow.

"Wait!" I holler again, blocking the way like the idiot I am.

Alyssa is almost to that row she stepped out of, attention on the magical staff.

"That isn't all. This isn't solely about Leo. Just

think what her equipment can do. The types of paranormal phenomenon each device can catch. In the dark."

"Exactly," Athanasius remarks. "She can catch everything." He is still very much determined as he eyes Alyssa, fingers tightening on his lit staff as he fights to restrain himself until I am done speaking.

Yeah, I phrased that part wrong, and I let it show. "Not what I mean. We can easily sneak around with that stuff, or pretend we are just making a movie."

Athanasius' staff flicks out a second time and he gives me an unsure expression. Then he nods, indicating for me to continue.

"Serina told me in that letter I found," I explain further, "how I have to protect this town. That I have to keep the magical world from being revealed to the humans. What if I do that by creating a…" I wave my hand in the air for a term. "… private investigation team. We can all work together. You, me, Jasper, and Alyssa."

"It will take time to go through classes and get a license for each of us," Alyssa chirps up.

I redirect. She is at the entrance of that row, but now she is relaxed and stuffing her video camera away.

"Also, if you haven't noticed, nothing is a secret in Stars Hollow. What good is it being a private investigator if everyone knows your business? Your every move? It is better to go under the guise of paranormal investigator and pretend you are just keeping me in check."

"No," Athanasius submits, at least after a few minutes of thought this time. "Your plan is to expose us." He is talking to Alyssa here, I realize. "You said so yourself."

Alyssa returns our way as confidently as she did at the start. "How about this? We work as a paranormal team and I only use footage that is debatable, this way I get exposure and this town gets tourists that will stay at my inn. Imagine all the antiques *you* will sell, all the food the *Thymes* will cook, and the touristy stones and potions that The Apothecary can create to drum up more traffic."

Those are good points. This town is dead, aside from the gossip that clearly exists.

Alyssa slips between me and Jasper as she did before and shrugs. "People will eventually come here anyway, might as well direct them into believing what they are seeing is just well-crafted attractions.

Everything else will be used to catch criminals and expose Leo Stonewall. We all get what we want in the end."

"I like it," Hawthorne interrupts.

Alyssa screams and nearly trips over herself as she jumps backward and away from the desk. Her finger comes up and points at the cat sitting by my arm. "He… he…"

Athanasius makes a face at Hawthorne. "That is extra duty tonight. And don't think I didn't see Robyn pet you after your incessant glaring. So double duty."

Hawthorne licks his paw and proceeds to groom himself. "Worth it. Her scream was priceless."

They Walked into a Park

"First things first," Athanasius begins as we each take a spot under the willow tree in the park. We all have a boxed lunch from My Father's Place. "No one, particularly the Stonewalls, can know about this half-baked scheme." The wizard still doesn't like the idea we set on, but he can see the usefulness of trying it out. "No one," he directs to Alyssa alone, "can know that you are aware of the existence of the magical community."

"Definitely," Alyssa nods quick and to point. Then she wiggles into the circle we automatically create.

The comment and reaction make sense, of

course. The magical community would not be okay with a human knowing they are here, and the Stonewalls would be so furious that not only would Alyssa be mind-wiped but most likely sent away. Jasper, Athanasius, and I would be punished – not sure how, but we would be. With that, I open my box and look down at my fettuccini alfredo. Sookie added four breadsticks and a small container of alfredo dipping sauce this time.

"With that said," Athanasius continues, finally opening his own box of biscuits and gravy with steak and fries. "Hawthorne must be with you for every trip," he points at the wizard turned cat in the center of our group, who just happens to have a rear leg in the air so he can lick his behind.

That is when Hawthorne's ears perk and his head shoots up. His eyes scan us as if he has just been caught doing something scandalous.

"As a familiar, he has abilities that no one else does. He also still has his wizardry magic. He will be able to get you out of trouble if necessary. And as he is under my command, he must obey you all until I say otherwise."

Hawthorne plops into the grass and rolls onto his

back, pulling up his front paws. He looks like a fluffy white bunny now. "Sheriff alert," he announces.

We all twist about, but I am the one who spots the man first as he makes his way over from the mechanic and hardware shop. He is in uniform, cowboy hat included. The only thing that looks off about the guy is the fact his face isn't fully shaved, although I think that look is in style. Something called *designer stubble*, which goes with his build – six feet at least, maybe a bit taller. Plus, he has muscles that make me think of...

Oh! All lights go off in my brain. *He is a shifter. The sheriff is a shifter. Well I guess that works in this town's favor.* The thought of what kind crosses my mind here.

"Hello, Athanasius," Sheriff Wolfe begins, stepping up to our group and looking down at us all. "Jasper, Alyssa." His gaze hits me last. "You must be Robyn."

I nod, forking up some of my pasta, and his name makes his species click. I mentally kick myself. *Wolf.*

"Getting settled all right? This town being nice to you?"

I am horrible at lying. I really am. Yet I nod again

and work with the truths I have. "Yes. Everyone here is amazing and so helpful." I indicate my new friends. "As you can see, I already made three friends."

I think my lie shows because Sheriff Wolfe frowns, but he says nothing about it. All he does is direct to Jasper, and here he reaches into his right pocket. "I found that cream I told you about." He pulls out a small jar with no label and hands it over.

Jasper puts down the cheeseburger he was about to take a bite out of and wipes his hands on a napkin. From there he accepts the item. "Thank you."

"I really am sorry about the allergic reaction."

I raise a brow, catching Alyssa do the same. Although *I* raise my brow at the way the sheriff maneuvers Jasper's wounds. Alyssa most likely is taking in the conversation, which shows when I glance over.

"This won't cure it, but at least the irritation will go down and you won't be rubbing and scratching. I am told you probably shouldn't be messing with your wounds anyway."

Jasper doesn't hesitate. He rolls back his sleeves to his elbows and opens the jar. He proceeds to massage the stuff on just as fast.

"Working?"

"There is a coolness to it," Jasper remarks, massaging his way along the bruises and burns further without looking back up at the sheriff. "It is nice."

"I didn't want to arrest you, Jasper," comes Sheriff Wolfe's next comment. It is easy to tell he speaks the truth. Something about the way his features sit after the announcement. "It was just that…"

"I know." Jasper twists the lid back onto the jar and slips it into his own pocket. "But the events cannot be erased. So just forget about it."

Sheriff Wolfe reaches into his other pocket here. "Your dad also wanted me to give you something. Not sure how to bring it up with others around so…" A little pouch comes out with two pills inside. "He noticed you didn't take them last night. You shouldn't miss a day."

Jasper claims the pouch. "I guess I forgot. Thank you for bringing them to me."

"I am supposed to make sure you take them," Sheriff Wolfe continues, straightening to his full height.

Jasper looks my way, then at Alyssa and Athanasius. "You really think I won't take them when I have witnesses here already?"

"I am told to make sure," Sheriff Wolfe persists. "Your dad is stressed over your health."

"Take them," Athanasius interjects, slipping a hand over Jasper's knee. His eyes say everything else needed. "You will feel better for doing it."

Jasper grabs his soda. "Fine." And he squeezes the pouch open and dumps the two little pills into his mouth. He takes a long drink next. "Now you can report to my dad that I am well and safe with friends."

If those pills are what I think they are, I am surprised Jasper is so annoyed by taking them.

"I will do that." Sheriff Wolfe's attention catches mine again. "I would like to stop by your house later today to chat, if that is all right."

"Sure," I say. "I should be home around 5:00." That is a time well enough away from now and before the events I hope to get to tonight.

Sheriff Wolfe tips his hat. "See you later, then." He waves at the rest of the group. "See you all around." He leaves, back toward the mechanic and hardware shop.

Silence fills the group. *I* don't even know how to break it, so I go to twisting up pasta and forking shrimp. I dip one of my breadsticks into alfredo sauce and take a bite.

"So," Alyssa ventures, "that comment Leo made on camera wasn't just an insult. You are a demon."

More silence. Jasper is ignoring the question as he munches on his burger.

"Apparently you can come out in the daylight," Alyssa presses.

I hate people who do that.

"You can eat real food, so you are not a vampire."

A smile escapes my lips. It hadn't even occurred to me that Jasper is a vampire going out in the daylight and eating a cheeseburger, but maybe being half human, he can.

"So what are you?"

"A vampire," Jasper remarks, and I catch amusement escape between chews.

"Ha, ha, ha," Alyssa faux laughs. "Mess with the human must be a fun game. Seriously, though, what are you?"

Athanasius grunts and covers his mouth to prevent food from showing.

Alyssa looks from me to Athanasius and back. "Are you two seriously going to play along?"

Hawthorne rolls onto his feet, getting all our attention. "He *is* serious. Jasper is an energy vampire, but he is also human."

"I guess that makes sense," Alyssa comments. "Being half human, he can go out in the day and eat real food."

Jasper's amusement grows. It is nice to see. "You watch too much television, Alyssa. "All vampires can go out in the day, although none of us sparkle. Blood vampires, however, prefer not to be in direct sunlight. Although you are right about the food. Full vampires cannot eat real food; they go out to hunt animals as feeding on people is illegal above ground."

"What is feeding like?" Alyssa inquires, tilting her head. She has completely forgotten her meal. "As an energy vampire?"

Jasper shrugs. "For me, horrible. I haven't fed the proper way since I was five when my dad asked my mom to take me on my first hunt. He refused to deprive me of my demon side despite me being indifferent about it. Then I returned home in tears thinking myself a monster and couldn't sleep for years after. I couldn't even go to school without breaking down. My mom stopped seeing me without warning, which made the situation worse. I have been on antidepressants since I was seven, which my dad could only pray would work on me."

"Oh," is all Alyssa can say.

Jasper sighs and his mood does this weird thing where it goes to sad and then nothing.

Athanasius again grips Jasper's knee, this time giving it a squeeze.

"My brothers, Azriel and Doger, however, find it exhilarating to complete the task the old-fashion way by digging their teeth into the poor animals rather than just absorbing through touch. I guess being around a century and a half in age, old habits die hard. They say it is like being high on drugs."

Mixed emotions fill me. The little story is sad, but fascinating. I want to question further, but at the same time worry I shouldn't. "Then how do you get your nourishment?" I almost squeak. This is actually why many think I don't have a filter, something to keep me from saying the wrong thing.

Jasper raises his burger. "The Thymes get this fresh for me. Makes me feel less guilty. The Cottonwoods, being Earth Witches, are the ones who fill my prescription every month, which is set at a much higher dosage than for a human."

"Wait," Alyssa shoots up a hand for attention. She almost waves it as her face scrunches and she takes a moment to think through whatever her next inquiry is. "Is that why you were arrested? The victim yesterday was drained dry and your pocket watch led Sheriff Wolfe to believe you went rogue?" Her eyes go wide from there and she gasps. "Are we hunting a killer vampire?"

And the connection clicks. Jasper's family is one of the possible two families we are investigating.

Emotions

I click away at the keys on my laptop, Coco curled asleep in my lap, and roll through another chapter of my latest epic fantasy novel. It is awkward, mostly because my computer has to sit on the arm of the couch. I am in the upstairs sitting room, with the light from the bay window shining on me from the left. You see, I am not allowed to sit at a desk even though I have an amazing one right next door in the computer room… Coco won't let me.

It goes something like this when I try sitting in a normal seat. Or even in the cushioned area of the window.

Me: [Stares at my screen as I read through my work and think of the next scene.]

Coco: [Somewhere in the hallway.] "Meow!... Meow!" [Can't see her, obviously, so I imagine her staring at the ceiling or doorway as that is what she does.]

Me: "In here, Coco!"

Coco: [Waddles in. Yes, waddles. There is no strut to her walk. Looks up at me.] "Meow!"

Me: [Stops editing and reaches down to pick her up.]

Coco: [Runs away.]

Me: [Goes back to delete a line I don't like and starts a new, better sentence.]

Coco: [Waddles back in.] "Meow!"

Eventually I do get Coco on my lap, but then she gets off two seconds later and starts the entire process over. Hence why I am on the couch. I wonder if I can get the house to magic a love seat into the computer room, but then my wall of self-published books and collectable doll corner will have to go elsewhere.

Oh well.

I check the little clock on the lower right-hand

side of my screen, which I have done countless times since I got home two hours ago. It makes me so nervous to have an appointment set and be waiting for it while I write. Anyway, it is 4:30, so half an hour left before Sheriff Wolfe arrives.

A knock at the door.

Or maybe he is early.

I stop typing and look down at Coco, who has one paw against the arm of the couch as if that keeps her from rolling over. She stares up at me in response, a purr vibrating against me, and she makes this face like she dares me to move her.

The knock comes again.

"I have to get up, Coco," I say. Then I click ctrl + S, saving my document, and close my laptop.

Coco leaps off, not in an insulted way but like something scared her. She is weird like that. In all honesty, however, I am surprised she didn't leap off when the knocking started.

The knock comes a third time.

"Coming," I holler so Sheriff Wolfe doesn't leave.

I lift my laptop and set it on the side table, then

head out into the hallway, down the stairs, and to the door all the way at the front of the house. I open it up, and on the other side is not Sheriff Wolfe.

It is Leo Stonewall.

Many swear words come to mind as I stare slightly up at the witch before me. That stupid face, stupid blond hair, stupid blue eyes. Who said he could look like Thor? He has no right to look like Thor.

"My grandmother asked me to bring this to you," he begins with no greeting, and something in his tone tells me he is upset. With me. That said, a large container appears between us that I hadn't noticed. "It was mentioned that you hadn't eaten dinner yesterday, and she fretted for hours until the exact meal you missed was remade and brought over."

"You didn't poison it, did you?" I blurt, lids narrowing. I don't even care I should have held that back.

He shoves it into my gut. "Just take it, will you."

I do, but only because Endora had it made for me.

"And next time you find the courage to use magic on me…" He glares the short distance down, taking a foot forward. Except there he comes to an abrupt halt and his gaze snaps upward at the doorway. Doesn't appear like he is going to finish that sentence. Or is it a threat? From there his shock turns into a smirk. "I see you have protection."

I spy where directed, catching sight of the horseshoe, satchel, and bells.

Leo runs the tips of his fingers along the doorframe, which spark. I am guessing from the spell I cast to link all the protected areas. He doesn't flinch. "Hm," he hums. He redirects.

And just then a patrol car pulls up, and out steps Sheriff Wolfe. Turns out he *is* going to be early. Thank goodness.

Leo steps away and plasters a fake grin to his disgusting face. "Have a nice rest of your day, Robyn." With that he turns and takes on the steps, nodding to Sheriff Wolfe as they pass each other. "Sheriff."

"Leo." Even Sheriff Wolfe has a fake smile, but he seems to be hiding something I can't figure out.

I watch Leo get in his Lamborghini, Sheriff Wolfe walk up my steps. Leo closes his door and I sigh.

"I guess I am too late," Sheriff Wolfe remarks rather solemnly.

I return to him curiously, and then I remember I

am holding food. I hug the container against me, wondering for real if it is poisoned. My curiosity about the sheriff remains, however.

Sheriff Wolfe points a thumb over his shoulder at the car that rolls away. "I take it you were just on a date?"

My eyes bug out. "No!" That may have come out loud and harsh because Sheriff Wolfe jumps. I shake my head with much determination, my goal to make this *very* clear. "He was just dropping off food Endora had made for me." I indicate the container. "I ate with the coven yesterday…" I realize that doesn't quite make sense only after I say it. "Except I didn't get to eat because, you know…" I shrug. "I am new and everyone had questions. I am not good with talking, or eating while talking, or any social…" I trail off. I am babbling things that are a secret.

Sheriff Wolfe grunts as he scratches his nose, but there is a small smile at the corner of his lips.

I blush. "Would you like to come inside?" I step aside so he can pass.

Sheriff Wolfe takes off his hat and ventures inside. "Thank you. I have always wanted to see the inside of this place, but Athanasius never let me in. Even during renovations." He turns to me as I close the door, and I gesture to the living room.

That is when Missy finally realizes someone is here and bolts through the electric dog door from outside with her high-pitched barking. In her old age, she is missing a lot. She used to bark the moment someone knocked or rang, although considering Leo had been here awhile and two cars literally came through...

Maybe the protection spell holds her back somehow.

Missy skids to a stop, squats in her submissive position, and goes in for a petting.

"Now what kind of attack dog is this?" Sheriff Wolfe speaks up as he bends down and gives Missy a scratch by the ear.

Missy starts doing her leg thumping and leans into the petting.

"She isn't," I comment. "You should have seen her the evening I arrived."

Sheriff Wolfe tilts his head and spies up at me from the floor.

"She went from aggressively barking at Jasper to screaming her brains out when he got too close."

A bushy brow goes up. "Poor Jasper. He is a nice guy."

I nod in agreement, Jasper's arrest on my mind. How can Sheriff Wolfe say Jasper is a nice guy if he arrested him without question? "Yes. He is." I purse my lips and hold out an arm confusedly. "So, Sheriff. What did you want to talk to me about?"

He returns to his feet, sending Missy into her rear wagging as her stub of a tail fails to move on its own. Her claws can be heard clickity clacking on the floor with all her excitement. "First off, you can call me Bane. I am off duty."

"Bane," I echo. "Like werewolf."

Bane brings his hat up to his chest and fiddles with it. "Shifter. Who told you?"

"Are you serious?" I ask dumbfounded, then I wave up and down his figure. "And your name, obviously."

He nods, still fiddling with his hat. "I guess it makes sense now why you openly said *coven* outside. Anyway." He makes his way into the living room at last.

I follow, Missy at my feet.

"I was wondering if you would be up for a date.

Maybe tomorrow night?"

That halts me, and I think back to his reaction toward Leo's presence just moments ago. I look down at the food I still hold; it is warm.

"I know this is coming out of the blue, and you are new here. Heck, we haven't really even spoken to each other. Our first outing doesn't even have to be called a date. We can go as friends and see where it leads from there."

I subconsciously squeeze the container between my palms. *A date? I barely know what to do when out with friends.* That gets my stomach fluttering, which somehow moves into my chest, and I redirect to find Bane waiting expectantly.

"I can give you time to think about it," he resumes. His hands come up defensively here. "I don't want to pressure you. It has just been me and my son for so long, and then you come into town." He gestures to me. "I figured, why not ask? What can I lose?"

Here is where I am definitely supposed to respond, but nothing comes out. I don't even know what to say. A date is a big deal, right?

Can't learn how if you don't try, my inside voice

offers. *Eventually you will have a first, and how else do you get one than at random?*

That is true, so I prepare to say *yes*. Until I think of all the moments I won't have with Jasper if I am with Bane.

Why am I thinking that?

Because my mother told me boys and girls cannot be friends. And once someone has a partner, you cannot be friends even if you are the same sex. You must give up friends if you want a partner.

"Robyn?" Bane interjects into my thoughts.

"I'm sorry," I say, blinking as I take in the man before me. A man I am sure many women would want because I have seen them swoon over similar ones in movies. "You caught me off guard." That is a partial truth.

"I really can give you time to think about this. We can set it up for a week from now, two weeks..."

I shake my head. It seems wrong to leave someone waiting for an answer, like I have to weigh all the reasons to be with them. But I don't want to lose Jasper.

"Is it Leo?"

The flutters cease, and now Bane has my full attention.

"Was what I caught outside…" He points out the window even though the blinds are closed, "… some sort of nervous encounter between you two? Well…" he seems to hesitate here, and it is odd on him. "… with you. Leo doesn't get nervous."

"Leo is a twat," I react. I slap my hand over my mouth, my lids so high my eyeballs are mostly white. But too late. It came out.

"Jasper," Bane counters. "I agree Leo is a jerk. Glad you see that."

My hand lowers, but I still regret my comment. "He's my friend." I am referring to Jasper here, but the word doesn't sound right. "My best friend." No, that doesn't sound right, either, which is bizarre considering I used it earlier in the day.

Bane nods. "You love him."

I just met him. The reply remains in my head despite my desire to point it out.

"I bet you are worried if you date me, you won't get to see Jasper. I can sense it on you right now."

I don't even have the compacity to absorb that

statement.

"You are terrified of losing him. Most women don't worry about that unless there is something behind it as a real man wouldn't make their girl stop seeing their friends. Even male ones. If he is truly just your friend, then…" He shrugs, hat against his chest.

"I'm sorry," I say again. What else am I supposed to say after being told I like a guy I just made friends with? No, love the guy. And from someone who just asked me out? There is also the obvious fact I am not attracted to Bane, which I feel I need to say sorry for as well even if I don't point it out.

"Don't be," Bane responds, stepping forward and making his way around me and out.

I simply twist on my toes and follow his motions around the corner and into the hallway. I am just within the doorway.

"Jasper is an amazing guy. He may think I hate him, but I don't. I have always stuck up for him and believed in him, and I will do so now. He will be lucky to have someone like you in his life." He stops at the door, hand grasping the knob, and turns to face me. "No hard feelings. But maybe we can still hang out as friends some time." His attention shoots down to Missy, who does that squat thing again as she inches toward him for another petting. "See ya, big girl." And he bends down one last time to give Missy what she desires.

He is gone after that, and I am left staring at a container of food I am now sure isn't poisoned if Bane could smell my emotions. Emotions I worry are going to make things very awkward. I can only hope the events of tonight distract me so I can deal with what to do about Jasper later.

Demon Section

A night vision camera is strapped to my hand. Another is strapped to Alyssa's. Alyssa also carries something she calls a ghost box that supposedly clears the air for ghost signals, an EMF reader, and an infrared thermometer gun. Jasper carries a notepad and voice recorder.

I want to say we are scouting vampire houses not ghost hunting, but why argue? We all did agree Alyssa could use anything debatable she could obtain, and when else would she get that stuff but now.

"Do I get something to use?" Hawthorne asks

Wands Upon a Time

once all the devices are out. "Maybe I should wear all black, too. Do you have a black cat sweater or something?"

I stare down at the fluffy white cat at our feet. He does stand out in the dark, but... "That would be suspicious. A cat wearing black sleuthing attire? And in the summer?"

"Maybe a small camera?" Hawthorne holds up a paw like his appendages can show us the size he means. "Do you have a small camera? How can I be a good cat burglar if I don't have a camera?"

"One," Jasper jumps in, finger in the air so he can physically count down, "cat burglars don't use cameras. Two, cat burglars are not actually cats. Three, we are not burglaring."

My forehead scrunches at that last word. "Burglaring?" I twist and squint to see Jasper better. You would think with his pale complexion he would be easy to see, but he isn't. He is like that moonlight that refuses to light anything up. "I don't think that is a word."

"Word or not," Hawthorne resumes, "who better to do it than a cat? And someone needs to get inside the houses unseen."

"We are not…" Jasper picks back up.

"That is a great idea," Alyssa interrupts as she rearranges her equipment on a new belt she has been excited to start using.

"What?" both Jasper and I sing as we dart are attention to the red head.

Alyssa makes an exasperated sound, entire body going into it. "We can't get proof one of these vampires is a murderer if we don't get inside the houses. Obviously, we can't just stroll inside if we don't know their schedule. When do they hunt? How long do they stay out? How well is their hearing? So…" She dramatically gestures to Hawthorne. "He is our ticket tonight."

"It is best *not* to break into a vampire house," Jasper states, shoving the notepad and pen into his back pocket. It is unlikely we need to handwrite anything anyway. "They can hear you for at least half a mile away, and they will be able to smell you on the air when they return. They will all be home tonight, though, as they only hunt on Mondays and Fridays. Today is Saturday."

"They can't smell me," Hawthorne states proudly, his little chest cutely puffing up. "I am a familiar, so I can hide my odor. Plus, my paws barely make a sound."

"They hunt animals," Jasper argues further as he stares determinedly down at the cat.

"Familiar," Hawthorne repeats matter-of-factly.

"Robyn?" Jasper turns to me.

"Yes," Hawthorne follows. "Robyn?"

I look from cat to friend and back. I even glance over at Alyssa.

"You know my opinion," the red head states. "But I am guessing you will be in more trouble with the magical community than me if caught, so it is up to you."

I rub my eyes and moan.

"You are not actually considering agreeing, are you?" Jasper asks me, his tone saying it all.

"If you do and tonight works out," Alyssa adds, "I will make sure to find a small enough camera for Hawthorne to use and order it. Right now, he will just have to remember what he sees."

My eye rubbing turns to whole face rubbing. "I must be insane, but it is my job to protect this town, so..." I redirect back to Hawthorne, hoping I won't regret this. "Be careful, don't get caught, and don't touch anything."

"Oh my gosh." Jasper turns away, but his form shows him slapping his forehead. It can kind of be heard, too.

Hawthorne scampers off with that.

Except we didn't set a time to meet back up.

"Wait!" I holler.

"Shhhh!" Alyssa hisses, finger up to her lips. "What is wrong with you?"

I cringe. "Sorry."

But Hawthorne stops and looks back.

"When should we meet up again? And should we meet right here?" Here is behind a tree on the lower east side between town, The Haunted Inn, and neighborhood. There are some surrounding farming fields.

"I think an hour, right here," Alyssa confirms.

Hawthorne bounds off once more.

"Since I have all the equipment…" Alyssa proceeds, adjusting her belt on her waist at last so she looks like an older Kim Possible. She wears dark green pants and a black top as well. "… and know how to use them, I will go off alone. I will focus on finding the ghost of the victim. I know what he looks like. You and Jasper can stick together and use the camera, recorder, and notepad to spy on any vampires out and about. I am sure Jasper can explain away your presence if caught."

"I can't, but sure," Jasper responds submissively.

"What do you mean?" I ask, nervous as heck now. Not only do we have Hawthorne breaking into houses, we have Jasper claiming he can't explain away our presence. "Doesn't your mom and your brothers live in this area? You said all the demons live in the lower east side?" The demons like to stick together while everyone else mingles.

Jasper gives an exasperated look. "I haven't been to this side since I was five. So twenty years. But I can just say I was showing you around and it got late, I guess."

"There we have it," Alyssa announces. She looks at her watch. It is 10:00. So we will meet back here at 11:00." And she struts off.

"I think she just likes to work alone," Jasper comments, and then he gestures with his head for me to follow. "That is fine. She can be impossible to be around."

"So Kim *Im*possible," I comment aloud not

meaning to, and I turn on the camera. I position it so hopefully my arm doesn't get tired, but it will.

"Huh?" Jasper looks at me funny.

I wave my thoughts away. "Nothing. Just an old Disney show about a red-haired girl named Kim Possible who fights evil. Nothing is impossible for her. She dresses like Alyssa, belt and all." *Or Alyssa dresses like her.*

"Ha!" Jasper exclaims.

I smile. His laugh is nice, and I find myself turning my face away to hide it.

"That is funny. I get it now. Kim *Im*possible. You know, I do believe Alyssa's middle name is Kimberly."

We enter the residential area at last, where I scan through the properties out of habit. Older homes are so beautiful. There I am caught by surprise. These are Georgian, which dates back before the founding of this town in 1860. In fact, Georgian homes are from 1714 to 1830, while Victorian homes are from 1837 to 1901. Is that possible? Did the founding witches break ground on demon territory? That sounds strange if demons are from the Underworld, but then who lived in these homes before the founding?

"The one on the right here is my mom's and her husband's. Their names are Maze and Trogus."

The lights to that house are all on, although white curtains are obvious as only shadows move about.

"They have lived in this area since the 1700s, in relative peace with the original Salem and Cottonwood Witches. The Stonewalls and Thymes came later. They built this home."

I take the house in more closely with that news, which is painted black with white shutters and white pillars. Its main part is rectangular, a smaller square part sits to either side. The door is dead center. I count three gable windows on the roof, five windows on the second floor, and eight windows on the first floor. The porch is a decent size with steps leading up to it. The yard is immaculate with its flowers and bushes and single tree.

I realize after this I subconsciously expected a Munster house. How stereotypical of me.

"The house on the left is another family of vampires," Jasper states as he points to a place just as we pass it.

Only a few lights are on in this house, and it isn't much different from the first except that it is in red.

"Four of them live together. Their eldest daughter moved in with my brother, Doger. His house is further down. The eldest son lives with a friend, also further down."

A crunch of sticks. I swoop the camera around and face the way we came with a lump that rises from my belly to my chest to my throat, but I see no one. Not even a squirrel. I check the camera screen here, heat rising along my spine, and wonder if maybe there is something beyond mortal sight. All I get is the eerie greenish view of night the lens gives off.

A chuckle. "So jumpy," Jasper interjects into my fear.

I rejoin him, chest thrumming, sweat I am not used to running down my skin, and we proceed with our trek down the road. Only now it feels like eyes are watching from every window. From every alley and corner. "I heard something."

"Well take a deep breath and let it out slow, your heartrate can be heard from half a mile away. Your sweat is even worse."

I do as instructed, sucking in a deep breath and letting it out slow as I convince myself repeatedly that

Jasper would know if people are watching. I do it several times before I finally calm enough to satisfy both of us.

"This is Azriel's home," he continues.

I look over, the curtains are wide open, and I swear I spot the silhouette of a cat on the inside wall. It is a living room I am seeing, and the light is from a shaded table lamp. I hope Azriel isn't home. Maybe the light is a trick to make people think he is home, except if anyone is watching it probably doesn't matter. Someone will see that darn cat, and us.

"So," Jasper sidetracks. "I didn't ask. How was the meeting with Sheriff Wolfe? What did he want?"

I scan all the homes around us, camera taking everything in. Many lights are out, many houses painted in dark colors. It is impossible to tell if my gut is correct about being watched. I just can't shake that feeling, even by convincing myself again Jasper would know. Even by telling myself I am just paranoid over this being the demon section. "He asked me out," I answer, listening for any peculiar sounds

Jasper's feet stop, but mine keep going. It takes two steps before I realize this.

I turn, camera angling right onto my friend. He

looks like a ghost rather than a vampire from this view, particularly on camera.

"What did you tell him?"

"Um." I think back to the meeting, biting my lip and blushing. I had hoped this event would distract me, but not to the point I would end up making our relationship awkward anyway. "At first, nothing. Then..." It is hard to look directly at Jasper, so I watch him through the camera and its green lens. Not sure that helps. I think it makes the situation worse. "Then he asked if I am interested in Leo, because Leo showed up before him."

"What?" Jasper looks beyond ghostly at this point. "Did he hurt you?"

I shake my head, shift my weight. I want to get back to "paranormal hunting".

But then Jasper swoops in and grabs my shoulders, practically leans me back and holds me in place. There he stares me straight in the eyes with black irises that seem to burn with fire.

I tense up, and suddenly I see my father before me sneering behind a beard. I forget to breathe. The man could do anything to me right now.

Then there is a growl in the distance, low and threatening, and I tense up more at the thought of what is out here with us.

"Don't lie to me. Did Leo touch you?"

I shake my head again, Jasper's voice bringing him back into view, and try to look elsewhere. But I can't. "N-no. B-but he was rude. He…" I gulp and try to remember who I am with before I forget. "He noticed my protection stuff and the spell. He touched it without flinching."

"But he couldn't get through, correct? He stayed on the porch?"

I nod and a part of me finally relaxes. "It stopped him in his tracks, but…"

"But?"

Leo's reaction. I hadn't thought much of it before, but it was so… "He didn't seem to care. It actually amused him. It was almost like…" And his eyes had gone grey that one evening, I quickly recall.

"He was going to find a way through."

I nod. "Then Bane showed up."

"Bane?" Jasper lets me go.

I rub my shoulders. Jasper had grabbed me pretty

rough. I hope it was unintentional.

"He asked you out," he directs back to the original subject. "You said *yes*."

My mouth moves to reply, but Jasper resumes walking the way we were headed. "That's great. He's a good guy. I am happy for you. I am sorry I grabbed you like that."

I don't move. Is this Jasper being jealous? That would mean he has feelings for me, too. That still doesn't make sense, although it would go with his reaction just seconds ago. Right? Not everyone grabs out of anger. And he said sorry.

Jasper gets further away, yet I still don't move.

"I didn't answer him," I blurt, not sure I said it loud enough.

Jasper stops.

"I almost said *yes*." A tremble in my voice commences. "How else am I to meet someone? How else am I supposed to know what to do on a date if I don't go on one? I have never been with anyone before, so like him I figured why not. But I failed to respond. No words came no matter how hard I tried, and the more I did try the more I thought about losing you. I don't want to lose you. I don't want to lose time with you by spending them with him."

Jasper almost twists here, but he pauses.

"Then when Bane finally asked about *you*, I couldn't convince even myself that we are just friends. It is strange, but he says I like you. Like, like you like you because you came to mind and stopped me from answering." I am not going to say love. Not yet. I am tired of telling people I love them and then they hurt me. "He noticed and that was that. He didn't even wait for me to actually give an answer, and all I could do after was apologize."

Jasper half turns at last. "You like me?"

I shrug. The words I am most used to saying (other than *I'm sorry*) come to mind. "I don't know." That is lame. I have been told even by my old therapist to stop it, and I know I have an answer. "I think so. I know you make me comfortable. I like hugging you. I don't mind you touching me. I worried about ending the day yesterday without seeing you one more time to make sure you were all right. I also don't want to lose you, and apparently that means something is there to worry about. But we just met and…"

Before I know it, Jasper is against me with one hand bracing my face. His lips are on mine.

I sag, his free arm catching me, and my heart stutters.

He pulls away, his dark eyes somehow darker, and he smiles. "Does that help you decide?"

My heart stutters some more. He has made my mind go blank.

Jasper grins broad and beautiful and dives into another kiss, which is much deeper.

I have to say, Jasper's kiss is one hundred percent better than being kissed by that boy back in high school. No, I didn't kiss that boy back, but his lips had felt cold, dry, and like... well... lips. Jasper's kiss, however... Jasper's is like a warm fall night. I swear he even tastes like burning leaves.

"Get a room!" a gruff voice booms.

We jump apart to find a man standing next to us, but something is off about him.

"Don't you see you are out in public?" He gestures to the neighborhood.

The man is average height, somewhat muscular, tan, with a short unkempt beard. He wears a blue and black flannel and blue jeans. I note cowboy boots, but no hat to cover his mess of brown hair.

"No respect," the man resumes shaking his head and crossing his arms, which is where I notice what is wrong.

The man is a ghost. He is on the verge of transparent; it is barely noticeable in the dark. Something in me is petrified about this discovery, another part excited. That excited part is what reminds me why Jasper and I are out here.

Shoot! The camera! I snap the device back up into position, having dropped it to my side. "Jasper, recorder."

The man narrows his eyes at me, and the exact point his face is supposed to turn red and his face throb is clear. Obviously the two last things don't happen. "What are you, recording me? You going to YouTube this?" With that he reaches out to snatch the camera out of my grasp.

I jerk away out of reflex, leaving the man's hand to glide through me instead of the camera. The action leaves an ice-cold sensation running up my arm.

The man freezes in horror.

"Sir," Jasper interjects, recorder at the ready. "May we have your name?"

The man looks at Jasper, takes him in a little at a time. "Donald. Donald Harris."

I don't know that name, but a glance over shows Jasper does.

"Well, Donald," Jasper takes charge. "I am sorry to tell you this, but you are dead. You died yesterday afternoon outside The Haunted Inn."

Dead Men Tell Tales

F ast forward is pressed with a bling. The camera flashes past the moment I bring the device up from facing the solid black shoes I wore and takes us all the way through half of demon section. My entire conversation with Jasper is passed over, but it does notably reveal the scene where I jump and spin around. There is also the noticeable point where the camera turns to Jasper and then drops to my side.

  Heat burns across my cheeks and shoulders and I spy at Jasper, who is to my left. Except I don't get a chance to see what he thinks because Alyssa presses play.

The camera now faces the ghost of Donald Harris, but the lens (night vision or not) doesn't catch him well. The man mostly resembles a foggy apparition bleached out by green. None of his features are visible, yet he is clearly male and the style of his clothes is decipherable.

"Jasper, recorder," camera me comes in, tone excited and frantic.

A crackly voice follows mine. It is Donald's, yet his words are difficult to comprehend compared to last night. Then his apparition whooshes forward, blurring what is decipherable of the man.

The camera moves with my jerk, the world on screen blurring along with Donald.

"That is so weird," I say. "He spoke as clear as day to us. He almost looked living."

"Actually," Jasper replies, "he was completely transparent for me. Probably because I am half human, but I could make him out pretty well. Even his words were off, yet fully understandable. I agree, though, this is strange."

"Sir," camera Jasper interjects, his recorder

comes into view on the small screen. "May we have your name?"

The apparition that is Donald blurs some more as it shifts back into view. It dances a bit as it settles into place.

I strain to hear.

"Donald. Donald Harris."

"Well, Donald," camera Jasper resumes. "I am sorry to tell you this, but you are dead. You died yesterday afternoon outside The Haunted Inn."

"I am dead?" Donald crackles through some more.

My forehead scrunches and my right ear tilts toward the camera with the extended effort I use to hear. I don't know why I am doing this. I know the entire conversation. I guess it is because I can't make out the words and it is annoying. I am not the only one, either. Athanasius does the same from his place behind his desk.

"Sorry," camera Jasper says. "But maybe you can tell us if you remember anything? From when you were at the inn? Maybe why you came to town at least?"

Donald's apparition dances and blurs again. This is where he panics and looks about, but of course the camera doesn't show that. It does, however, show how he dims, like he is about to ditch us.

"Donald," camera Jasper presses while remaining calm, "stay with us. Tell us what you remember so we can help."

"I... I." Donald's apparition drifts backward and almost vanishes off the screen. He had faded into transparency, at least for me, pretty bad in real life, too, but he at least remained visible enough that he could be identified.

"Donald, please," Jasper continues. "Whoever did this to you is still out there. Whoever it is might kill someone else, possibly many."

Donald's voice crackles. No one who wasn't there would know what he said, which is clear when both Athanasius and Alyssa look to me and Jasper with imaginary question marks hovering over their expressions.

"My truck ran out of gas," Jasper translates over.

"Hm, so an outsider," Athanasius interjects.

All our eyes go back to the screen. I am sure everyone thinks the same as me. Other than myself, the first outsider, and now he is dead.

"I drove all day and night for three days straight until I got to this area," Jasper resumes to translate with each crackle of Donald's voice that comes through. "I sure hoped to get further, but oh well. I ended up walking into town. This place is sure far away from the road. I was exhausted by the time I arrived, so after filling my container I decided to stay and rest."

Donald drifts back toward us, and once more his apparition only reveals minor details. Maybe his distance from the camera affects his voice, too. Could have been his faded state as well.

"I checked into The Haunted Inn," Donald's words start up as I expect, leaving us straining as before since Jasper is no longer needed. "I got settled and went out to eat, and then…"

Donald's smokey appearance does that dance and fades. I vaguely recall this moment as obvious frustration, at which point Donald grabs his head with one hand and closes his eyes. Again, not on camera, just in my head.

"I think… someone grabbed me. I remember feeling hands. Arms. There was a sharp pain to the left side of my neck, and another on my right collarbone.

Then nothing." Donald's apparition steadies to my surprise and for a moment I think he solidifies on the screen. This is where he calmly looks from Jasper to me and back. "I guess it makes sense now, why everyone has been ignoring me. I couldn't even get a meal at the diner. I guess it also explains why I keep waking up out here rather than in my hotel room."

"Out here?" camera Jasper asks. "Where exactly. In front of this house?"

I turn the camera to point at said house.

"No. Down the street. Two more houses on the right."

"That is Doger's and Belial's place," Jasper comments since it is unclear where camera us stands at the moment.

"I have also woken up in front of another house elsewhere. It is white with green shutters and a green door. Victorian rather than Georgian. Actually looks freshly painted. Loads of flowers and bushes and a large tree."

"Sounds like Jaxon Michaels' home," Alyssa chimes in from my right. "He recently painted and planted some new flowers. Although his grass needs mowing."

Donald's apparition fades and is gone. It goes much quicker on screen than it had in person.

"What just happened?" camera me asks.

"I think he just moved on," camera Jasper replies. "He finished, without realizing it, his last piece of business."

Alyssa presses stop and closes the camera.

"Sounds like we have to talk to Doger and Belial?" Athanasius begins.

"And Jaxon Michaels," Jasper adds. "It is weird a human is involved, but why else appear in front of his house?"

"I don't think talking will help," Alyssa states as she packs away her video camera. "Murderers aren't going to be like…" She waves a hand and sarcastically rolls her eyes. "… oh, yeah, that guy. Yeah. I killed him."

I purse my lips and think. This is complicated. From there I lean into the desk and cross my arms over it and all the stuff that is spread across its expanse.

"Also," Alyssa continues, "talking to people will draw attention to us, and then we will never be able to solve anything because this entire town will know our every move. Criminals will learn to hide better."

If only I had seen the murder like I had seen the fire at the diner. My thinking stops right there and I gasp quite audibly. My gaze falls on the storage room door as I picture that moment clearly, bringing in all the facts I know so far about that moment in time.

"What?" everyone asks at once.

The murder and the fire were both at 12:30 in the afternoon on the same day. But what does that mean?

"Robyn?" Jasper's hand slips over my shoulder.

I turn to him. "The murder and the fire were both at exactly 12:30," I repeat aloud.

"Yeah, so?"

"I had a vision of the fire in the diner at 12:30, but not the murder."

"You had a vision?" Alyssa asks. At first she sounds surprised, but then… "Cool!"

"That is peculiar, though," Athanasius comments, drawing all of our attention his way. "A fire over a murder? I would think a murder would be worse. Serina always had more important visions over minor ones."

I hadn't thought of that part. Maybe there is

something in that. "It wasn't just a fire," I muse aloud so all can know my train of thought. "Sam couldn't put it out. It was going to be an explosion. The entire diner was going to blow and kill everyone inside."

"More people, more deaths," Jasper adds in. "So the fire was considered worse."

I look to him and nod. "Yes." I return to Athanasius and Alyssa. "That seems strange, right? Two major events that result in deaths happening at the same exact time, but I only see one of them? Maybe someone knows I have visions and planned both the fire and the murder for 12:30."

"That is a stretch," Jasper interjects further. "That person would have had to know about your visions before you. That was your first."

I turn back to Jasper, my sails knocked off course.

"Since you haven't met or seen Doger, he couldn't possibly have planned around you. As for Jaxon Michaels, he is human."

"Maybe the house Donald found himself in front of wasn't Jaxon Michaels' but someone else's," Alyssa offers.

Wands Upon a Time

Well now, there is something.

"Maybe Donald simply noticed that one first and forgot he woke up in front of another. Who lives near him? Are any of them in the magical community?"

I look from one face to the next, as I personally have no clue. I haven't met everyone yet.

"I do believe a family of witches does," Athanasius responds after a time. "A shifter, too."

"But now the question is why?" Jasper asks. "Why would someone in the magical community kill an outsider? Someone they don't know and have never met?"

I think about that, and I catch all around me do the same. Fingers go to chins and tap, lips purse, eyes shift up to the ceiling.

We all forgot one crucial detail, however.

"Donald was drained dry," I offer up. "That still leads us to a vampire, and Donald pointed out Doger's place."

"That is right," Athanasius says, pointing a finger at me.

"But why appear in front of a non-demon home?" Alyssa asks. "Is it possible more than a vampire is involved?"

"He said he went to the diner," Jasper comments. "Maybe we should talk to Sam and Sookie, see if they interacted with him. Or if *he* attempted to interact with *them*. If he went right after his death, maybe he remembered something then that he didn't remember later."

"That is a good idea," Athanasius concurs. "Particularly if the fire was intentional to distract Robyn. We should also see if we can bring in the Thymes. They are agreeable, and we may need at least one other witch on our side."

"But I thought that wasn't a good idea?" Alyssa asks. "I am not supposed to know about you guys."

Athanasius nods. "Yes, well, the Thymes are an exception. And I am thinking it is wise, now that I see the extent of this team of ours, to have more than a witch, a wizard, a half-demon, a human, and a cat familiar."

Hawthorne! I look around. I haven't seen the cat today.

"So when you guys head over, make sure to talk to them about our team and see if they are up for joining. See if they can meet with us this evening, too. Here, for a ritual."

"Ritual," I inquire, rejoining the conversation.

"Yes. I actually have one planned for later. It will be an easy one to rule out suspects."

To Keep a Secret

"Soooo," Alyssa draws out as we pass Bejeweled.

I stare through the clothing store window from my spot sandwiched between Alyssa and Jasper. The shop makes me feel angry as the owner lied about me and Jasper being in there. Only I don't see anyone inside. Not even the owner or assistant.

"When is the first date?"

"Huh?" I direct left to find Alyssa staring at me with a knowing expression, but I am confused.

"I think she means the kiss," Jasper offers up.

I direct my attention toward... *What is he, my*

boyfriend? That isn't important right now, but his mess of black hair is because it hides his eyes today and for some reason I am enjoying looking at it. And there it clicks.

Alyssa watched the entire footage, listened to every detail of our conversation last night. The kiss may have not been on camera, but it was obvious based on context.

"Oh!" I am sure my face is lit up like my brain.

"I personally would not have turned down Sheriff Bane Wolfe, but…"

I redirect back over just as Alyssa shrugs.

"To each their own."

"Then why don't you date him?" Jasper suggests.

Here we stop outside the diner.

"I have seen you drool over him."

"I might. Do you think he likes the Kim Possible type?"

I think I am having an aneurysm. I forgot I said that, and I can't believe I hadn't even processed the fact the camera had been rolling.

"Or is it the Kim *Im*possible type?"

"I'm sorry!" I whine. Then I cover my face to

hide my horror. "I didn't mean it as an insult." I honestly don't think I meant it as anything. She made me think of Kim Possible.

"No problem. I like Kim Possible. Good show."

I drop my hands. It doesn't sound like Alyssa is upset. In fact, now that she has my attention again, she waves one hand over herself.

"You know how long it took to find clothes like hers? I honestly think they created her off some image of me."

What kind of response does she want from that?

She shrugs again. "Any who, how about I bail on this part as it might look suspicious for all three of us to be talking to the Thymes. Not sure how many in the magical community will be watching and taking notes."

"All right," Jasper and I say together. Not a bad idea. Probably best anyway to bring her up with her not present. Most people start attacking the one who doesn't belong, never letting a word in edgewise.

I know that reaction well, and the feelings that come from it.

Alyssa heads back the way we came, but she keeps going past Broomstick Books and Antiques. I guess she is heading back to the inn, which makes sense since she runs it and may be getting guests soon.

"Where is she going?" Hawthorne interrupts.

I snap my gaze down to the fluffy white cat familiar as he strolls up to our feet. It is like he appeared out of nowhere. "Where have you been?" I ask instead of answering. "We had an entire meeting without you."

"Spying," Hawthorne sits on the sidewalk, eyes slitting. He looks between Jasper and me. "Where is she going? We have work to do."

"Most likely to sift through the footage more," Jasper replies. "As for work, right now we are headed inside the diner to talk to the Thymes." He opens the door with that and waves me in. "Ladies first, as always."

My Father's Place has more people today. Half the place is filled. I note Bane sitting at the table Jasper likes, and he spots us and waves.

I wave back.

"There's Sam," Jasper says.

I glance around quick and find the man in question taking an order. How did I miss him? There is someone else, a male teen with sandy brown hair, in an apron behind the bar.

Jasper's hand slips along my back and he guides me over. Hawthorne swishes against my legs as we make our way, arching his back like any normal annoying feline. He makes sure to meow, adding to his act.

"No cats," Sam says just as he leaves a set of customers and comes toward us. He points down with a pencil. "The hair gets everywhere."

"Awwww," a customer sings, "but the cat adds to the place. He is cute."

"Yeah," someone else chimes in.

Sam shakes his head and sighs, and we meet each other halfway.

"We aren't staying," I say, hoping that helps. I take in the place again, pretending to be absorbing the old sixties-style setup. There is even one of those wall menus behind the bar I hadn't noticed my first time. In truth, I am looking for the two who spoke. "Can we talk, though? Sookie, too?"

"Sure." Sam turns to the teen behind the counter. "Brody, take over the tables." He gestures to the back door. "Come."

I spy Bane again. The sheriff is reading a newspaper now, which he holds up so it doesn't touch his sandwich and coffee. He is the only one at that end of the diner. But something tells me he is watching. I can't exactly put a finger on how I know, but he is watching.

The swinging door opens, and in we all go. Sookie is hard to miss inside as she waves a wand here and a hand there. Spices fly through the air and spoons stir. I can hear sauces sizzling nearby and water boiling. And for the first time I am awed, and I must know how to do this all myself.

"Sookie, dear," Sam calls out.

"Hm?"

"Robyn and Jasper wish to speak with us. Can you halt your cooking for now?"

Everything stops or flies to a safe spot. Sookie walks over, grabbing a rag along the way to wipe her hands.

"So?" Sam returns to us.

I forget, and I turn to Jasper. My mind is whirling with what I just witnessed.

"Well it is a loaded conversation," Jasper begins.

Sam pulls out his wand and four folding chairs slip in from unknown places. "Take a seat."

"Well first off," Jasper begins, picking a spot close to the door, "there is... well was... a ghost."

"A ghost? We have a few around town, Jasper. You know this. My daughter knows this."

"Well this one..." I claim a spot between Sookie and Jasper. We are in a small circle and our feet almost touch. "... said he came here after he died. He didn't know he was dead, so he came here to eat and..."

Sam makes a face that he understands, mouth open wide. "Yes. I recall that. A ghost did come in here. It was shortly after you two left."

"Is that the one who stomped through here yelling at me?" Sookie asks as she reaches back to fix the bandana that holds her thick hair. It is green today.

Sam nods. "Mhm. Such an angry thing. I had to banish him from this place because he sent several dishes falling and shattering in his rage. There was going to be no talking to him. It was the best I could do on my own. I meant to bring it up with the coven and have him sent off to the next life, but I forgot. Why, what happened?"

The swinging door opens, and we all twist just as a profoundly serious Bane steps inside. Or maybe I should be referring to him as Sheriff Wolfe. No one can get more serious than this guy right now. I think he is in work mode.

"Yes," Sheriff Wolfe says.

Uh oh.

"What happened? Please enlighten me." The swinging door swishes closed behind him. "And maybe you can add why you three…" He indicates me, Jasper, and Hawthorne," were skulking about the demon section last night with Alyssa after curfew."

The curfew. I forgot. With that, what I had prepared to say if caught slips my mind.

"You are lucky I didn't arrest you all for breaking and entering, since you figured it was okay to send Hawthorne into every vampire home in town. Just because you aren't *burglaring*, as you all quaintly put it, doesn't make it legal."

I *knew* I heard something. He was probably behind us in wolf form the entire time.

"Why didn't you?" Hawthorne asks from his spot on the floor between me and Jasper. His head is eerily twisted around and tilted back to view the huge man in the doorway. "We spent a good hour out there. You could have even done it while these two here were making out in the middle of the street."

My jaw drops.

Both Thymes stare at me wide-eyed, but it may be over the fact Alyssa is involved more so than the kiss. Maybe even due to the fact I let Hawthorne sneak into several houses. Or maybe all three.

"Did you enjoy that view?" Hawthorne adds.

Sheriff Wolfe holds up a palm. "That is beside the point. The issue here is that I saw *you* two..." He eyes me and Jasper specifically, "videoing and recording an apparition. You saw and spoke to Donald Harris. What did he say? Can he remember who killed him?"

I shake my head, sure whatever excuse I had wouldn't have worked on Sheriff Wolfe anyway. "No."

From there, Jasper and I take turns explaining everything, with Sam patiently listening. Sookie doesn't have time, or patience, so she goes back to her magical cooking that is hard to ignore.

~*~

Sheriff Wolfe leans sideways against the wall, away from the swinging door that Brody (a young Kitchen Witch) rushes through from time to time. His brows are together, his forehead is scrunched, his arms are crossed. That looks very much like anger.

Oh boy. I realize then shifter anger, from what I read and watch, is worse than human anger. Something to do with the animal side of them. But I always believed animals, particularly dogs, could see and hear spirits. It sounds like Sheriff Wolfe can only see apparitions.

"Sookie and I will keep this a secret and help as much as possible," Sam jumps in when it is clear no one is going to speak.

It has been five minutes maybe. I could be exaggerating. Hearing someone finally say something, though, and in our favor is a relief.

"As a member of the coven, and a founding witch family, I personally agree with all decisions and steps taken to this point. Sookie and I will definitely be at Athanasius' after we close up. Is 6:30 all right?"

Jasper and I exchange a look. I personally don't see why that time would be inconvenient. I look down to Hawthorne from there, just to see if he has anything to say, but he is cleaning himself thoroughly.

"6:30 is fine," I say.

"I want to attend," Sheriff Wolfe interjects gruffly. "As this meeting is in regards to an active homicide with no solid leads, I need to be there. And from now on you inform me of everything, every move you make that affects my job and this town, and I will make sure no one realizes what you guys are truly up to. It benefits me anyway. This town is insane with gossip."

Now *that* I didn't expect, the sheriff to secretly hire us as his personal investigation service. I feel like Monk now. But paranormal Monk.

Pendulum

On a notepad, I write a list of names Jasper gives me.

Each one is spaced two lines apart for tearing.

    Maze

    Trogus

    Doger

    Azriel

    Remiel

    Lazikeem

    Belial

    Nero

    Modeus

Wands Upon a Time

Abaddon

None of these vampires have last names, but I am told that is no big deal as that just means they are full names.

I go ahead and add Jaxon Michaels at the bottom, a human. Weird, but Donald had said he woke up in front of this man's house. Neighbors are eliminated as this list would be far too long due to needing to include every single name of those directly next door and those across the street. Also, most of the neighbors are human as well. The closest magical beings are a tiger shifter and a witch family with children in school. There is also the fact that Donald passed on after detailing Jaxon Michaels' entire property.

"Add Jasper and Alyssa," Sookie speaks up as I get ready to tear.

I look at her, stunned. Jasper is so close to me I can feel his body tense, and I think I hear something rustle from somewhere on the desk I am leaned back against.

Sookie holds up a hand. "I like you, Jasper. I don't believe you did it. It is just standard procedure to use all names of all suspects, even if we believe they are innocent. This way the list isn't biased."

"And you are using my name because?" Alyssa asks from the other side of our large circle. She is sitting next to Bane, her hand purposefully close to his knee.

It is Sam who answers. "You have video of Robyn using magic, and honestly I never trusted you. You sneak around a lot with your equipment, and last night you intentionally went off alone."

Alyssa twerks her lips, but she contains any further argument.

"I want to make one hundred percent sure you aren't going to turn on us. So once we have the names of the murderers, I am going to have Robyn ask another question in regards to who not to trust."

Alyssa shrugs. "Fine." Here she flips her hair and side-eyes Bane.

"Maybe unknown as well," Bane chimes in. "It is possible all the names on the list are wrong, or only some of them are correct."

I jot down unknown. "I will go ahead and rip the names out and put them in a circle," I say then. And that is what I do. I rip one off and place it in a spot on the floor. I rip another and place it next to it.

"Mix them up," Sookie says, "so there is less likelihood the pendulum will be swayed to a particular name."

"All right." I go to move them.

"While at that, flip the names over," Sam adds, halting me. "This way no one sees the names. Also scramble them after they are all on the floor to make the results more honest."

I nod as I place the two torn names randomly upside down on the floor, then proceed with tearing, flipping, and dropping rather than organizing. Why bother organizing if I am going to scramble. This takes no more than a minute. Another minute to get all the names tossed about and placed in a perfect circle.

I have to have the circle perfect, and no one questions it to my relief.

"Since you have never done this before," Athanasius speaks up. "Let's make this a small lesson." He sweeps out a small wooden box from behind him and opens it up. Inside are six different colored pendulums and several chakra stones. But then here he looks to Bane on his right. "Is this fine with you?"

Bane grunts affirmation. "She is new and there is

honestly no hurry. So all good."

Athanasius pulls out a purple pendulum and holds it up so it dangles for all to see. "This is amethyst. It is a healing crystal. It helps the body's immune system eliminate toxins." He sets it aside nice and neat and pulls out a blue pendulum. "This is sodalite. It is used for wisdom. It inspires logical decisions and pertinent questions." That goes to the side as well, the start of a row. The third pendulum to come out is pink. "This is rose quartz. It is for love. It is for reconciliation and making good decisions in times of crisis."

I wonder here if the wizard will have me pick a pendulum to use. So far sodalite and rose quartz sound appropriate, maybe sodalite more so.

Athanasius pulls out an orange pendulum. "This is golden healer quartz. The stone for spiritual connections and healing. That is pretty self-explanatory." And he sets it aside with the others. A black one is up next. "Smokey quartz. It draws away negative energy from a person, place, or thing." It goes aside. Finally, a yellow one. "Citrine. The well-being crystal. Good for food and allergies and spritzing up your home and life."

I look along the row of pendulums as that last one goes down. I am still set on sodalite.

"Which one do you think we should use, Robyn? Which one will help in this situation?"

"Sodalite?" It comes out as a question, and for some reason I think my answer wrong even though I was confident about it seconds ago.

"Good."

I relax in relief, not realizing I had tensed in the brief moment.

Athanasius claims the blue pendulum and hands it across the circle to me. He scoops up the rest and puts them away.

"So how this works..." Sam jumps back in.

My eyes take in the color of blue that makes up sodalite as the cool silver chain runs through my fingers. It is mostly a dark blue, but there are swirls of light blue and white. It may seem like I am not listening, but I am.

"... is you hold the top of the chain, steady the stone center of the circle of names, and ask a specific question. For example, 'Which name is involved with the murder of Donald Harris.' You cannot specifically ask the pendulum to name the murderer as there could very well be more than one involved in this case and the pendulum won't know what to do. It is best just to repeat the process with a well-thought-out question until all names are revealed."

I figure that is it, so I take the chain at the end like I have seen on Charmed and prepare the magical device over the circle.

"Make sure to clear your mind," Sam resumes before I can release the stone to dangle freely. "Think only of the question and nothing else. Don't even think of the names under the papers. Just the question and your desire to know the answer. Do not verbalize. Those around you shall do the same, keeping the circle clean and locked from all that is outside it as it will be drawing from us all."

"Sometimes your own energy is needed," Sookie chimes in. "If the pendulum doesn't move, that is. When this happens, just focus on what is inside you and pluck out just a little bit and send it forth through the chain."

I release the stone, eyeballs locked on it and how it sways ever so slightly. *Which name is involved in the murder of Donald Harris?* I make sure to phrase that perfectly, one word at a time so there is no confusion.

The stone remains mostly steady dead center.

Which name is involved in the murder of Donald Harris? I repeat.

Steady still.

I try not to get frustrated but rather close my eyes and breathe slowly. Here I imagine a light inside me. Not sure if that is correct, but images of meditation always show a light right at the core of a person.

To my surprise – yes, I am surprised – a light appears. It is bright and white, although I can see a streak of black running through it, and the stuff fills the space all around me. Warmth emanates from every inch that I can feel. It takes everything in me not to acknowledge that black streak, though, and just pluck from my light. With that I let what I take spill through me to the chain.

Which name is involved in the murder of Donald Harris? I ask a third time.

The chain between my fingers twitches. It is moving.

I open my eyes as Bane claims the small paper the pendulum hovers diagonally over.

"Jaxon Michaels," he reads off. "Well that complicates things."

"Proceed with the second round," Athanasius interjects.

I do as request, steadying the stone so it can start anew. Then I go straight into myself rather than waste my time simply asking the question. I find my light once more, pluck a piece, and…

I didn't even ask this time. The chain moves.

Bane grabs this piece as well. "Doger."

"That can only mean Belial as well, right?" Alyssa asks, her gaze moving through the group.

"Don't," Sookie blurts with much irritation. "Keep your mind clear as well, remember? The circle must be a safe place for the ritual."

"Right. Sorry."

I go again, this time not even needing to do anything. The stone moves the moment I let go.

Bane again grabs the name.

"Belial."

Another round. I sure hope this is it. We don't need another suspect to investigate. Another murderer on the loose. That makes me mentally kick myself.

The pendulum goes to unknown.

"Four people?" Jasper jumps in.

It is safe to say we are done, so I gather up the chain and stone and relax my arms into my lap. *Unknown can't be a result of my thoughts, could it?* "Two vampires, a human, and an unknown," I say aloud to sort out that unnerving question. "That unknown is not a vampire because we have all the names down. So who could it be?"

"I don't think it matters much," Bane comments, standing up.

Alyssa pouts as she stares up at the sheriff.

"Donald was drained dry of his energy. His very life force. That is Doger and Belial, no contest. They are the ones I need to focus on nailing to the wall. If we can get Jaxon Michaels and whoever else is involved, great, but they didn't murder anyone. They were most likely accessories in some way, shape, or form. I hope you don't mind, but I need to get going and see if my pack can help uncover anything about these two."

"Pack?" Alyssa squeaks, her enamored attention still on Bane. Then her face lights up. "Ooooo, a shifter. What kind?" She looks ready to wiggle and kick like a child on too much sugar.

Bane stares at the red head for a second, then

walks off into the chaos that is Broomstick Books and Antiques.

"I don't think he is interested," Jasper smirks. "Maybe you laid it on too thick."

Alyssa sticks her tongue out at Jasper.

"Now, none of that," Athanasius lectures. "Sam and Sookie want one more ritual."

All the remaining members move to close off the spot in the circle that had been Bane's as Sookie reaches over and gathers up all the names, scrambles them once more, and organizes them anew. "There."

I think of the first question, how to use that to form my next.

Which name cannot be trusted?

I take the chain as before, steady the stone center, and close my eyes. It is much harder not to think about who can and cannot be trusted, and then I wonder if the question is clear enough. Obviously the four selected before cannot be trusted.

"You are hesitating," Sam comments.

"I am not sure the question is clear enough. We may get the same names." I open my eyes and look around, arm at the ready and stone still in my grasp.

Everyone exchanges looks.

"That is true," Athanasius comments. "There is no way to frame this question unless we remove the names drawn during the first ritual."

Alyssa does that. She flips every name over, draws out the original three (not the unknown), and jumbles up the rest. The circle of names is smaller now. "There!" she sings.

I close my eyes again, dive into myself, and release the stone.

Which name cannot be trusted?

The stone remains steady, but I can't help but think it should move to unknown for Leo. Or maybe it doesn't because he isn't "unknown".

A Good Day Gone Wrong

The Thymes stick around while Alyssa ditches us right away. Saw that coming. The outcome of the last pendulum ritual didn't sway any opinions, so it isn't a surprise when I catch Sam and Sookie shake their heads as we all watch Alyssa disappear around the shelves and stack of antiques.

"She is nice, you know," Jasper states. "She has been kind to me growing up and has accepted me being a half-demon. She may come off a bit strong at first, but it is a defense mechanism. Give her a chance."

Sam shakes his head again and crosses his arms.

"She is nice, but she may very well ruin this town. Even if unintentionally."

"Then why agree to let her work with us on investigating," I ask confusedly.

The bell chimes Alyssa's exit.

Or maybe this is the start of the Thymes rethinking this investigation business.

"As you said at the diner," Sookie comments, "the humans are coming anyway. And as we see it, Alyssa can't be kept in the dark no matter where she lives. She is too curious. Her eyes are always watching. Might as well have her on our side to help us keep magic a secret for as long as possible."

I look back to where I last saw Alyssa. I honestly don't know what to think about her. I neither like nor dislike her, but what I do know is that I doubt she will be the one to ruin this town.

"We should get going," Sam resumes. "Let us know if you need anything else. We will be glad to help." With that he heads out with his daughter in tow.

"Mind assisting me with some sprucing," Athanasius asks.

I turn just as the wizard indicates his desk area.

"That isn't sprucing," Jasper interjects. "It is more like unpacking an entire house."

"I agree," I respond, not that I don't want to help. "It is also late. We won't get even half of this done before dark."

"No worries," Athanasius says, directing his attention to the chaos and noticeably taking note of where to begin. "There is honestly no point getting the entire area organized anyway. More stuff will appear by morning. Hawthorne wasn't entirely lying about this place changing daily."

My head cocks slightly at those words. "What?"

"I have to echo that," Jasper adds. "What?"

Athanasius grabs a stack of stuff ranging from books to letters and begins sorting through them. It unburies a few small knick-knacks. "This place seems to attract lost books and antiques. In all my five hundred years, I have been unable to figure out why. I gave up on the store itself, but my desk and back area I try to keep up no matter how pointless."

"Hey!" Sam's voice rings through the shop.

Now that I think of it, I never heard the bell chime their exit.

"Yes?" Athanasius hollers back.

"There is a medieval cookbook here my daughter wants."

"Take it! You can pay me later!"

"Thanks!" Sookie responds.

At last the bell chimes.

I look to Jasper and mouth, "A medieval cookbook?"

He lifts one hand as a way to say, "Don't ask me." Then he grabs a pile and sorts.

I grab my own pile, noting strange titles. I can't make heads nor tails of them. That gets me to direct my attention to the pictures and symbols to help me sort. Many of the books suggest some bizarre old techniques for medicine, theories about the earth, religions long gone. There is one book I think is a novel, but it is hard to say as the cover only has an image of two serpents in a circle like they are eating each other's tail.

A quick open and I see I can read the language, but the words are not English or Spanish. It is the Witch Language. A novel in the Witch Language.

"You can have that," Athanasius says. "I know you like books, and that one I know for a fact is entertaining."

I nod and set it aside, coming to an assortment of old letters. The brown kind with writing you can barely read because it is so swishy and fancy.

This is how it goes for over an hour and a half. Except it doesn't look like a dent is made when finished. I think Athanasius is confused on when items appear because they secretly did while cleaning.

~*~

And just like that it is sunset, only there are no clouds in the sky so everything slowly dims to a grey as the blinding sun drops along the horizon. Have you ever noticed the word sunset doesn't go with blinding sun and grey? Colors come to mind.

"Thanks for helping out," Athanasius says from the doorway of his shop, his body holding the door open wide.

"Not a problem," Jasper and I say together.

I giggle and blush, then take in the vacant town just as Jasper clears his throat to hold back his amusement. Not a soul is in sight.

"Maybe you two can stop by tomorrow and help some more."

I hug my new book to my chest as I consider what time to stop by. The smell of the old paper within the binding is strong and wonderful. "I can do that. I can be here at 10:30."

"Me, too," Jasper concurs. "It can be our first date."

I look over, and that black mass of hair is in his eyes again. A lot of it is sticking up now, though.

"Of course, we will have lunch in the park later. Just you and me."

"Hawthorne told me you two were an item," Athanasius says. "I wondered when it would happen. You two are good for each other." That is when the little bell above the door chimes, signaling it is about to close. "Have a great evening."

But screaming ends the evening before it can start. It rolls across the expanse around us like the very air, the sound as high-pitched and loud as the ringing of the clocktower.

My insides leap out of me I am sure, and I catch Jasper leap as well as he spins to face the town.

The screaming pauses for a second, and then picks right back up.

"That doesn't sound good," Jasper states.

Obviously. I scan the town frantically, trying to pinpoint where the screaming is coming from, and spot Hawthorne bolting at full speed from the opposite end. Just off toward the south a bit, from what looks to be some sort of barn converted to a dance studio. I can tell it is a dance studio because the double doors are wide open, although there is no sign to name the place. There I watch as the cat familiar runs across a lane, the single car out and about just missing him. Then he bolts across a strip of grass, makes his way across the next street, scampers through the park, and finally joins us.

The cat familiar isn't even panting.

"Murder," Hawthorne blurts. "Behind Tabatha's Studio."

"As in Tabatha Stonewall?" I ask, recalling the eighteen-year-old. *She has her own studio?* But that is beside the point. There is a murder, so I tuck my book under my arm to get it out of the way and get ready to take action.

"Yes. Her parents bought her the place. Now there is a woman dead behind it, drained dry. She smells terrible and Tabetha is screaming bloody murder."

"Let's go," Athanasius takes charge, letting his door slam shut as he steps out instead. From there he leads the way. "Better for us to get there before someone else."

It is hard not to agree with that idea when little bells start chiming from every direction and feet begin stomping across pavement.

"What is going on?" someone calls out.

"Is it another murder?"

"Is someone *being* murdered?"

Athanasius picks up his pace. "Hurry, you two."

Jasper grabs my hand, sending tingles through me, and we start jogging. I can already see those closest to the dance studio making their way over. I don't think we are going to make it before them.

Until I see a wolf in an alley. The animal bolts into a shadow and within seconds a man steps out. He is blond and built like Bane.

"I need everyone to stop and stay where you are!" he hollers, his voice barely making it over the screaming as his hands come up for attention.

No one listens. They just keep going, their chatter seen and no longer heard.

Another man slips from an alley, this one also obviously a shifter, but with dark brown hair, a beard, and a deep tan. "Everyone needs to stay back!" this one booms.

Everyone stops.

"Who do they think they are?" some man says close by enough that his words make it to my ears. "Sheriff Wolfe lets some of these guys have too much control. Might as well hire them as extra deputies."

Grunts of agreement all around as the screaming stops once more, then resumes.

"Where do you three think you are going?" The bearded one asks, drawing us to a stop with one swift motion into our way.

Athanasius points to Tabatha's. "We are helping Sheriff Wolfe," he breathes low.

The man looks to the other, who nods, and we are allowed passage.

"What the heck! They get to go through?" a woman hollers insultingly.

"They are friends of Tabatha's," the blond states. "She called them for support."

We fly through the entrance, and Tabatha

immediately falls into a heap of tears on the floor near a back set of doors leading to an enclosed grassy area. Athanasius immediately slides to her side there, pulling her in and hiding her from view, while Jasper and I leap beyond and onto the crime scene.

It is definitely a woman this time. One who can't possibly be more than thirty-five just from her facial features and body structure. Her hair and skin, however, tells another story. Her hair is pure white, her skin so translucent it can't be real. And her eyes are wide open and empty, left staring into oblivion with a mouth wide open. Looks like she died of fright. Pure fright.

"Linsey," Jasper says, and he covers his mouth.

I cover my eyes, not wanting to see the scene anymore. I don't even know why I wanted to see it to begin with. Is this what draining a person dry of their energy looks like?

"All right," enters a tough female voice from behind.

It is here I let my hands slip as I twist. The woman entering the dance studio now is tall and athletic, but definitely human. She is dressed in a deputy's outfit.

She stomps on over, showing her authority. Her

name tag reads Huckly. "Which one of you found the body?"

Tabatha squeaks, but Athanasius remains hiding her.

"I am going to need to speak with you once you are ready." With that she fixes steely eyes on me and Jasper. "Were you two here when she found the body?"

"She called us," Jasper replies. "Most of the screaming you heard was the phone call."

She nods. "All right. Stay out of the way then."

She shoves by us, sending us off to the side, and finally Sheriff Wolfe enters.

I step back into the studio, Jasper along with me. I don't want to be out on the crime scene anymore anyway.

"Gosh, I can smell her," Sheriff Wolfe comments in a low enough voice for only us to hear.

"So can I," Jasper states. "I say around 12:30."

Sheriff Wolfe nods as he continues his way over. "I agree. But it could be that she was in the sun awhile. The last victim had been in the shade and didn't smell as bad."

"12:30?" I echo, looking from Jasper to Sheriff

Wolfe. That is the same time as the first murder, and the fire.

Sheriff Wolfe takes on the threshold out the back and vanishes before I can comment or think much else. No joke. The doorway literally vanishes right behind him, the little grassy area with them. The entire dance studio with its vintage barn structure even goes along with them all.

Oh boy. I recognize this immediately and go with it, taking in how the old barn walls are quickly replaced with that of one of the shops and a tall wooden fence. The grey sky is above me, only it is hard to say exactly where I am. All I can decipher is that I am in an alley behind a shop.

I sniffle involuntarily, my hand going to my nose and rubbing it without me asking it to do that. Then I spot a large black dumpster opposite me.

Gosh the thing reeks. The flies are even difficult to ignore.

At last my attention lands on a figure in a dark grey hoodie. The hood drapes over the person's face, putting him in shadow. I am sure whoever it is, though, is male based on his stance and square torso. He has his hands in the front pockets of his outfit.

"I can't do this anymore!" a young male voice begs. I can hear the onset of tears trying to garble the words. A teen, it sounds like. Something about the tone vibrates through me, as if I am the one screaming. There I am filled with terror and guilt over murders I did not commit. "You got what you wanted! Now keep up to your deal and leave me and my friends and family be! I don't want to go down for murder! I am only sixteen!"

Laughter. The hooded man is laughing. His shoulders shake with the intensity. "Dear boy," he says, confirming his sex, "did you truly believe I would let you go? That your friends and family were safe from me?" He slips out a hand, one in possession of a black-hilted dagger with an intricate design on the blade.

I gasp. No, the teen I am seeing through gasps. We back up as one with that, the hooded man stealing steps forward with each of our movements. Our back hits the wall, eyes widening, and we watch the dagger rise into place between us.

Athame, the boy thinks into our minds. *Where did he get that?*

The man plunges the dagger into our gut, the pain

is unsurmountable, and all goes dark before I can even let out a sound. The last thing I remember is the wall sliding along our backs, the taste of blood, a chant that would never work as the man is human, and then…

Arms.

"Robyn?" Jasper whispers into my ear.

I manage a gasp and a small sound that has no term for it.

"Robyn, it is a vision. Open your eyes. You are okay."

Another gasp, from forcing my lids open. My hands are clutching my belly. I look down, but there is no dagger or wound. I am back in the barn/dance studio.

"Robyn?" Jasper presses further.

"A boy," I breathe. "A teen. He is going to be stabbed."

A man, not unlike the two shifters outside, runs in and out the back. He doesn't acknowledge us or say a word.

"Where?" Jasper asks.

I push away, shaking my head. I can still feel the dagger plunging through me over and over again as if on constant replay, and I grip my belly once more. "I don't know." I look to Athanasius for help just as the wizard hands a slowly calming Tabatha a handkerchief.

"What did you see?" Athanasius asks.

I think back. "A dumpster. It smelled horrible."

"That could be the diner or café? Maybe even OneStop." Jasper interjects.

I twist to see my boyfriend better. He is sitting crisscrossed about halfway behind me, just enough to still be at my side. "Do either of them have a sixteen-year-old male teen working there?"

"The diner," Athanasius blurts. "Brody." He nudges the air in the direction out. "Go. Now. I will stay here. I will let Bane know."

~*~

The stares as Jasper and I run through town for a second time are relentless. The whispering, relentless. One would think people would have better things to do then spy and gossip, particularly when there has been a murder.

But I guess people just can't help but stop to see what happened, even if it is a car accident on the side of the road. Everyone slows down or stops to get a look.

Then a hand grabs my arm and pulls me to a halt.

Ripping me out of Jasper's grasp. It is Samantha Stonewall. "Is my daughter all right? Did you see her?" She glares at Jasper here, but quickly returns to me with a gaze demanding an answer. And her blue eyes, which could pass for ice, turn a smokey grey.

Like Leo.

Like... a Dark Witch? I have no clue.

"Yes, but..." I force my gaze away and toward My Father's Place. "I am really sorry, but I must go." I tug to get out of her hold, but she has a firm grip on me that tightens. "I saw a murder. A young witch is going to die."

Something tells me to say witch instead of boy, as if Samantha would not let me go otherwise.

Samantha releases me and takes off as lady-like as she can through the crowd that may very well be the entire town. Just imagine what this place would look like during a holiday gathering.

Jasper reclaims my hand, and with what feels like two bounds from a standstill we are venturing between My Father's Place and Bejeweled. We round the corner left with that and into the back alley.

But Brody is on the ground already, in a pool of

his own blood. I can tell he was stabbed more than once. One of those times in the chest.

I saw the murder as it happened. Or likely moments before like the fire. And just like that I am crying, slipping down to my knees because I can't hold myself up and process this unfairness all at the same time. Plus, I am realizing I didn't see Linsey's murder, which had been around noon today when nothing else was going on.

"Get her out of here," a gruff voice that could only belong to a shifter booms through.

Jasper grabs me under the arm, taking the book I have clutched in my hand, and lifts me up. Then he gets up alongside me and we waddle out of the alley.

"It is not fair," I moan. "I saw the murder, I should have been able to prevent it. Capture the killer."

"Maybe it was meant to be," Jasper says as we break back out into the open, but he pauses us just at the threshold.

Everyone in town is, obviously, still spread throughout the park and street, waiting expectantly for news.

"Maybe there are some deaths you are not

supposed to prevent."

We make our way right, along the diner windows, and inside. The little bell chimes our entrance, and Sam comes out from the back.

"I thought I locked that. Is everything all right?"

"Brody is dead out back," Jasper says as we make our way to the closest table, "and everyone is swarming the murder of Linsey at Tabatha's."

Sam bolts, dropping his rag, and is out the kitchen door and gone.

"We even got definite names," I continue to think aloud, moments flashing by as I take a seat with a plop. There I stare at Jasper in disbelief. "We got names, visions, a ghost who told us what he knew. All this was supposed to be done and in Bane's hands." *How did this whole day go so wrong?*

"I know," Jasper replies, reaching under the table to touch my knee. "I know, love."

Now this is too much, and I drop my head into my hands and just stare down at the table.

Not Going to Let This Go

Sheriff Wolfe struts into the diner at the exact moment the sun vanishes from the sky, bell chiming his entrance. But it is the way the door opens with the force only someone his size can make that tells me it is him. About that same time, Sam and Sookie come in from the back with lids that had shed tears.

My head remains in my hands and my eyes on the table.

"Is she all right?" Sheriff Wolfe asks.

I drop an arm and shift my head along the single hand that now holds it up to look at the tall, bulky man towering over me just feet away. His cowboy hat is in his grasp, up against his chest.

Athanasius finally arrives here, sending that bell chiming some more, and falls in next to the sheriff.

"I saw and felt his death as it happened," I say in a monotone, dried out of all emotions. "I experienced his last moments." This is the only explanation to what happened almost an hour ago. I thought about it hard. If Brody had died moments after, then Jasper and I would have seen his attacker go into or leave the alley.

"That makes sense," Athanasius comments as he finishes the distance between us and sits across from me. There he reaches over and pats my hand that rests on the table.

I direct toward the wizard man in disbelief, which gets Jasper to claim that free hand and squeeze it gently. The way Athanasius said those words… He knows something I don't.

"Serina intensely experienced the surroundings from her visions if the events were happening at that exact moment," Athanasius explains. "She would lose herself, forget where she truly was and who she was with because what she was seeing was no longer subject to change. Events that were moments away yielded *some* sensory aspects, but they tended to be confusing as she felt herself *and* the victim. She could clearly differentiate between reality and vision, forcing both timeframes to collide in her mind due to the close proximities and the limited space to interfere. She never registered much of anything if the events were days or weeks in advance, and they came in flashes – like memories."

I take time to process that information, and then to process that I am just learning this. That leads to the fact that no one had warned me about visions. Athanasius hadn't even been surprised when I told him about the fire. "You couldn't have told me that before?" I state with my continued monotonous tone. "Why was I left to learn about this ability all on my own?"

"I was forbidden to help you in this area," Athanasius reveals, his expression dropping from its already somber appearance to an even more somber one. "Serina requested that you come into your psychic powers on your own. That is how it has always been from one Salem witch to the next. She said self-learning connects your mind, body, and spirit better, allowing your third eye to show you all it can. If you are taught from the start, then your mind is being molded into what it should do. How it should react to the world and visions. Next thing you know your mind puts up barriers that takes unlearning to tear down."

I shift my head again, this time so my hand covers my eyes. There is nothing I can say anymore.

"Did you at least see the attacker's face?" Sheriff Wolfe asks from behind me. He hasn't moved yet.

Even Sam and Sookie are still standing close by.

Hawthorne has vanished again, I realize.

I shake my head. "No." My voice sounds weird for some reason. It didn't earlier. I figure it must be my position, then I realize everyone is silent. "He wore a grey hoodie."

"Did you see the weapon?"

I almost shake my head again, out of habit at this point and the desire for this horrible week to be over, but then stop and sit up. I twist to look at Sheriff Wolfe once more. "Yes, actually. Brody mentally called it an athame. It had a black hilt and some sort of design on the blade."

"So another witch," Sam interjects.

I turn to the Thymes, shaking my head many times until I am sure my brain is rattling. "No. Human.

When the man chanted, Brody clearly thought, 'The chant won't work. He is human.'"

"Chant?" Athanasius echoes. His curiosity is brighter than the lights hovering above us.

"It was in English," I clarify. "Something short. I don't remember the words. I was so scared. He was so scared. It is almost like he never spoke them, but I know he did."

"Can you try to remember?" Sam jumps back in, an arm going around a dazed Sookie.

Sookie is standing there like she turned into a statue. The air conditioning makes her thick black hair move slightly under her green bandana. Her hair is the only thing that moves on her.

"Try," Jasper encourages, grabbing my hand with both of his here and massaging it. "Close your eyes and think back."

I prepare to do just that, a heavy sigh escaping. Only that sigh is followed by a sudden rise of panic that grips both my belly and chest. I think I might start hyperventilating. Before I know it, I am trembling. *No.* I shake my head with that and take in the people around me, but looking at any specific individual makes me desperate to scream in agony. "I..." my head shakes again, my breath catching in my lungs. "... can't. I died with him. I..." I shake my head a third time, tears welling up to blur the room. "I'm sorry, I can't."

Sheriff Wolfe's palm appears on my shoulder. I am not fond of so many people touching me at once. Handshakes are hard enough. One person is hard enough. I am still surprised I am okay with Jasper touching me. "That is all right, Robyn. If Brody's murderer is human, and what he thought is true, then there is no reason to know the chant."

"I can't even imagine a chant that can be translated into English that would be used with an athame," Sam comments further. "Even wand magic uses the Witch Language. Any English versions are useless. In fact, athame's usually require a ritual. I am guessing whatever spell this man tried to use was obtained from the internet, from some wannabe Pagan/Wiccan group."

I let another heavy sigh escape, this one much louder, and my shoulders slump. There I recollect the entire vision without meaning to. It is like my brain, even though just seconds ago told me it can't handle this, decided it isn't a bad idea to retrace all its steps. So I force myself to stop… and right when Brody screams his plead.

The plead.

My eyes go wide as all the names from the pendulum ritual returns.

"Robyn? What is it?" Athanasius asks.

"I think I know who the unknown name is," I say, all the pieces clicking together. "It is Brody. His murderer is Jaxon Michaels."

"How do you figure?" Sheriff Wolfe inquires, moving forward at last and taking the remaining seat at the small table. This puts him with his back to Sam and Sookie

I mentally go over that plead, make sure I recall it correct, and nod to myself to begin. Except I need one more second to collect myself as I tend to rush when public speaking or reading aloud. One student in a class I subbed once said I read like a boring YouTube video. "Because Brody's last words were, 'I can't do this anymore. You got what you wanted. Now keep up to your deal and leave me and my friends and family be. I don't want to go down for murder. I am only sixteen.'

From there the man..." I pause, imagining a face I can't possibly know. "Jaxon Michaels," I correct, "said he never planned to let Brody or anyone go free."

"Go down for murder?" Jasper repeats. "Unless Brody is referring to future attacks, this must be a reference to Donald and Linsey. What are the odds that our little town that has been locked down for one hundred and twenty-five years will have multiple murderers at once?"

"It doesn't connect," Sookie finally chimes in, although her dark brown face is rather pale at this point and she is still staring off without blinking. "How is Jaxon Michaels connected to Doger and Belial? A human, a witch, and two demons going on a killing spree doesn't make sense. The first two killings are also done by a vampire, only Brody is done by a human. And why kill Brody anyway?"

"Well," Sheriff Wolfe responds as he twists to see the Thymes, arm going along the back of his seat, "Brody, from what it sounds like, was killed for trying to back out."

"No," I respond, drawing attention back onto me. That thinking is wrong. "He would have died anyway."

"I am guessing his attempt to get away," Jasper adds, "got him killed sooner. By the way, Brody's family is Jaxon Michaels' closest magical neighbor. They share a fence."

Sheriff Wolfe uses the table to help him stand. There he leans into it in thought.

"I also just realized," Jasper continues, "that Brody's girlfriend, Delilah, works at Bejeweled. Her mom inherited the place, in fact. Her grandma is the one who turned the building into a clothing store with the idea of making garments from nature for those who prefer naturally made items. Sara is the one who brought in the styles from out of town. He may have tipped them off that a human is blackmailing him, so they lied to protect themselves and their business."

"I wish I could use all this," Bane comments, straightening, "but I am afraid I can't. I can't even send my pack into that neighborhood as it has more humans than any other. Even one wolf could get someone out the door with a gun."

"Can't you get a warrant?" I ask. "Samantha Stonewall is a witch so…"

Sheriff Wolfe cuts me off with a negative grunt.

"There is no physical proof. Proof within human means. I can't just say, 'Someone had a vision of Jaxon Michaels killing Brody'. I can't say, 'We did a ritual that drew out Jaxon Michaels' name'. I definitely can't say, 'The ghost of Donald Harris described waking up in front of Jaxon Michaels' house after he died.' Even in the magical world there has to be proof to back up this information; even if that proof is recreating rituals or bringing in the ghost himself." He steps away and walks to the door with that.

Rage fills me. Jaxon Michaels, Doger, and Belial are clearly murderers, and we can't do anything about it. "That isn't fair."

Sheriff Wolfe halts, hand almost to the door. He doesn't turn. "You are right. I know more than anyone. As Sheriff, it sucks knowing I can stop criminals without much hassle. Then I remember a good portion of this town is human and they have no clue I am a shifter, that their mayor is a witch. Even Deputy Huckly has no clue. Thank you, though, for all the help so far. Best to stay out of it from here." And the bell chimes with the weight of the door opening.

No. I am not going to let this go. I am Robyn

Salem, and Selina made it clear what my job is as a founding witch. With that I lean back into my seat and think. How can I use our paranormal team to catch Jaxon Michaels, Doger, and Belial? How do I prove they are working together?

"What is that look in your eyes?" Sookie ventures. "You aren't planning to defy Sheriff Wolfe, are you? He was pretty mad last time."

I suck on my bottom lip and smirk. "He said he can't send his pack into the human neighborhoods. That means he is going to have demon section covered and will need help with Jaxon Michaels' end."

"He said he doesn't need any more help," Jasper states. "We gave him all we can. Our part is done."

That is when Hawthorne jumps onto the table. Wherever he came from, I don't know. He seems to disappear and reappear as desired. "Shush. She has a plan, and I want in."

I smirk wider. I wonder how hard this next part will be.

Amateur Sleuthing

We are packed into Alyssa's car (me, Jasper, Hawthorne, and Alyssa). I am in the front with Alyssa, Jasper is in the back with Hawthorne. The plan had been to use Jasper's vehicle, but his father needed it to haul some stuff for a customer – I am still baffled they share. From in here, just around the corner enough to see the entire street, we stakeout Jaxon Michaels' home.

"I can't believe I am agreeing to this," Jasper says after five minutes. "I can't believe I convinced my dad to give me today off for this." That is right, he told his father the truth.

A few children run by laughing, making us all duck down fast. I hear the peddles of a couple bikes.

"We are going to get caught."

We all sit back up slowly, eyes scanning for more children. Or their parents.

"Although worse can happen on a first date."

"We will be fine," Hawthorne replies. "I can cloak us all at once. Or we can have Robyn cast a spell on each of us, but that will take time and will wear off in fifteen minutes. Her spell, however, will allow us to be separate."

"I am up for you cloaking us all," Alyssa states. "We only need it to get in and out, and if we get stuck inside it is best not to be tied down by a fifteen-minute invisibility spell. We can always gather together and stand perfectly still, move as a unit. I also don't like the idea of not being able to see each other."

"Mmmm," Jasper moans uncomfortably, rocking into his seat in the back and inhaling so deep his chest puffs out. "Do you really think it will take more than fifteen minutes?"

Chatter. There are two teens coming our way from behind. I can see them from the rearview mirror.

"Duck," I say.

We all go down.

"All clear," Hawthorne announces this time. I notice him in the side passenger mirror peeking out the rear window. Then he moves to look out the window behind me. "And I see Jaxon Michaels getting into his truck."

That the man is, and he pulls out of his carport and heads the opposite way. Jasper said he would, as he backseat drove us to this corner that sits near a field.

"Let's go then," Alyssa resumes as she opens her door.

I follow suit, but I note Jasper hesitate. Jasper moves so slow that Hawthorne decides to leap to the front and go out my side.

All our doors close at once, the sound reverberating off the metal frames until it shakes the glass, and drifts into the air.

I flinch and quickly scan around like a startled deer. I don't notice anyone watching; I even check windows.

"See," Jasper whisper hisses. I know he is talking to *me*. "Even you are scared."

"Group around me," Hawthorne instructs. "Now. Before someone sees us."

I scan around the ground to find where the cat familiar is and locate him at my feet. It is seconds later when both Jasper and Alyssa join us, Jasper slipping his hand into mine and intertwining our fingers.

"Perfect," Hawthorne declares. "We can begin moving. Just don't step more than five feet away and don't talk when people are close enough to hear."

"That is it?" Alyssa asks.

"Yep."

With that we move as one onto the street and make our way to the opposite side. Jaxon Michaels' house is smack dab in the middle to the left.

"I think we should go in the back door," I comment as low as possible, afraid that even someone across the street can hear us even from inside the house.

"I agree," Jasper says.

We maneuver beautifully, like we have done this a thousand times, and make our way across the tall grass that is Jaxon Michaels' lawn. The blades rustle under our shoes, making me flinch again and dart my gaze around. I am sure it looks quite odd to have grass moving when there is no breeze. But again I see no one, not even children. Although children most likely would be too distracted to see anything strange.

At last we reach the gate, which Alyssa pries open, and we all squeeze through. She closes it once we are all gathered securely on the other side.

"We are safe now," Hawthorne comments. "No need to stick together."

We all nod in unison and head around the house. It doesn't occur to me no one knows how to pick a lock until we reach our final destination.

"Maybe it is unlocked," Alyssa says, reaching out.

It is, not to my surprise I find despite my previous thought. This is a small town, and I am sure even minor crime is so low no one locks their doors.

The door squeaks open. The hinges are rusted. Obviously if a man can't mow the lawn, he can't check the doors. Although he did plant flowers and repaint, so maybe the grass and hinges are next.

The noise, however, brings a realization to mind. "He does live alone, correct?" It is just that I think there is a high chance, in a small town like this, that Jaxon

Michaels isn't single. If he is married, or partnered, his lover could be home and hear us come in. He could even be divorced or widowed and have children.

"You are just asking that?" Jasper replies, his tone saying it all. I don't even need to look over to see his face.

I blush. "I have never done this before."

Hawthorne goes in first, shoving his way through like a true cat. Alyssa is second. Jasper and I let go of each other so we can follow.

This is a small Victorian. I didn't really take that in from the outside having been worried about getting caught. Now, though, I can see a small sitting room to my left, a small dining to my right, and straight ahead a mudroom. I don't think I have ever seen a mudroom at the front before.

I march along behind the group, spying a door about halfway down the short hallway – the bathroom – and it is directly under the stairs to the second level. The kitchen (big enough for one) is visible from here with its breakfast nook in the tower portion. After the stairs is the study.

"I will take upstairs," Hawthorne says and trots

up the stairs.

"I will help," Alyssa responds as she trails behind at a walk.

"I guess I will do the study," I say to Jasper with a shrug that sends my arms out. Then I head in.

"I will keep look out," Jasper finishes, entering the study with me and heading to the window that outlooks the front lawn.

The desk is my first goal. I am not exactly sure what to look for that will prove Jaxon Michaels is a murderer, but the desk is a good place to start. All sorts of things can be in a desk. Right?

I make my way to it and around. The seat is up against that front window so the desk faces the shelves of encyclopedias. There I pull open the middle drawer.

Pencils, pens, erasers, some odds and ends.

I go for the top drawer to the right.

Notebooks, each are solid black with a silver Christian cross. These look promising, so I pull them all out and set them on the desk side by side as they were in the drawer. From there I open the first notebook, and inside, on the first page, I see the word *SPELLS*.

My eyes go to the desktop computer that is

pushed far back. It practically touches the end of the desk. It is an old one with the bulky screen, tall tower, flimsy keyboard, mouse with a cord, and wires all over the place. I don't see a printer anywhere.

"How old is this guy?" I ask aloud.

"Around forty-five. Maybe fifty. Why?"

I flip the title page, having expected this to be spy notes or something, and find the first spell. Or rather curse. Whatever it is, it gives me pause. All I can do is stare at it for several long moments, maybe an entire minute, as I don't know what to make of what I am seeing. It is most definitely a curse, I conclude. A curse to make horrible things happen to someone. There is a drawing of a voodoo doll underneath and how to make it while chanting. "These could have been printed or put into bookmarks to save time writing them all down and drawing the pictures. Do voodoo dolls even need spells and curses?" I am mostly answering Jasper's question at this point as I am still at a loss for words.

"Huh?"

I close up the notebook and set it face down so I know it goes on top. "Jaxon Michaels has a notebook of spells, and the first requires a voodoo doll."

"I am not sure. Will have to make note to ask Athanasius."

I grab the next notebook, that cross on the front making all this ironic. A Christian using black magic. I suppress a laugh and open this next book to the title page. There is a desire to know what I am getting into before I see everything for sure. Not clear what I expect, though, but it definitely isn't *POISONS*. Either way, that intrigues me. I imagine instructions on how to mix a potion with things that have peculiar names, are from some reptile, or are a piece of a mummy. That all gets me to flip to the next page fast.

ACONITE/WOLFSBANE/MONKSHOOD. There is an actual piece of the plant dried to the page. From there it details how to grow it, how fast it works, what potions to put it in, and who to use it on.

"What the bloody hell?"

Jasper rustles against the curtains. "Hm?"

"This book has deadly herbs in it."

"We don't have that here," Jasper responds. "Jaxon Michaels would have had a massively difficult time locating the stuff and having it delivered. Now, maybe easier."

"Apparently Jaxon Michaels figured it out because…" I turn, gently tilting the book so Jasper can see. "This is aconite."

"Oh!" Jasper exclaims. "Wow!"

"The Apothecary doesn't sell this stuff?" I ask as I close the book and set it face down on top of the first.

"No. They don't sell things that are innately dangerous. Obviously, some things can be used for evil, but they can also be used for good. Cynthia makes sure to cleanse everything from estate sales before putting them up on her shelves. Anything truly dangerous gets destroyed."

I take up the third notebook and open it up. *WHO IS WHOM.* I go to the next page without thinking.

There is an old polaroid of Athanasius pasted to the top. His full name is in bold beneath that: ATHANASIUS CONSTANTINE. Next I read: Wizard, Male, Five-hundred-years-old, 5'6", Broomstick Books and Antiques (Place is cursed), Lover was Serina Salem, No known allergies, Killable (Proved with a cut).

Something in me is afraid of the next page, but I flip.

BANE WOLFE. His human and wolf images are

included. Now that is a shocker. Werewolf (Shifter? HAHA!), Male, Thirty-years-old, 6'2", Sheriff, Pack Leader, Son named Thaddaeus (Ten-years-old), Wife named Sierra (Deceased at age twenty-three), Allergies include wolfsbane, Killable.

That gets me to close the thing immediately and gather all the notebooks.

"What are you doing?" Jasper demands.

"I am taking these." I hug them to my chest, regretting not bringing my messenger bag. I left behind my fanny pack to avoid dropping buttons but didn't think of bringing an evidence bag.

That is when Jasper's hands appear around the notebooks and attempt to rip them from my grasp. "You can't," he says, his tone level. "They are evidence."

I jerk away with a glare.

Jasper glares in return from behind his mass of black hair.

"Oh yeah, and how will we get Sheriff Wolfe and Deputy Huckly in here to find this *evidenc*e? Might as well take them with us and figure out how to use them to corner Jaxon Michaels."

The roar of an engine pulls into the driveway. A

truck door slams. Alyssa's feet are heard racing down the stairs.

My heart nearly stops as Jasper's hands fall away from me.

"Hurry," Hawthorne hisses. "Get around me."

I close the drawer, and then Jasper and I race over to the bottom of the stairs as the notebooks slide in my grasp and get jumbled. I see Alyssa has some folders.

Then a key slips into the lock, the front door squeaks open.

We race through the house to the back door, it is still open, and we stumble out. There Hawthorne swishes his fluffy white tail and by a miracle the door closes silently.

"Let's get out of here," Alyssa whispers. "I found old type pictures, the kind that automatically print out, that prove Jaxon Michaels spied on Brody and blackmailed him. Delilah is in some of them."

"You found that upstairs?" I comment in surprise. Why wouldn't that be in the study?"

She nods as we start venturing around the house to the gate. "Yes. It was in his bedroom. It overlooks Brody's house."

That makes sense now.

We open the gate and once more squeeze through until we are all out on the other side. Alyssa closes it much more carefully this time around to keep the latch from making too much noise.

And that is when we spot a cruiser pull up to the house. Deputy Huckly gets out, stops, and looks at the truck. She cocks her head and then gets on the radio hanging from her shoulder.

I dare not breathe. I can tell no one dares move. If Deputy Huckly had been Sheriff Wolfe, we would be doomed because I can feel my heart beating. He would most likely also smell our sweat.

"Alice?" she radios over.

That must be the secretary.

"Are you sure the caller said Jaxon Michaels' place?"

Silence, in which time Deputy Huckly puts a finger to her ear to indicate an earpiece.

Jasper nudges my shoulder and gestures onward, so I look to Alyssa and Hawthorne to confirm. With that we set forth, and Deputy Huckly moves toward the house. Yet it seems so much further heading back to the car. Like somehow the street grew while we were inside, or the house moved to the furthest corner. This makes the moment we are finally free to get away for good much more of a miracle than the backdoor closing in silence.

We all scamper to our respective sides, breaking free of Hawthorne's protection, and collapse into our seats with a sigh of relief. Hawthorne is so relieved as well he is in my lap, leaned against my front.

"That was close," Alyssa comments.

"Sounds like Leo called it in," Jasper says. "Alice stated on the other end Mr. Stonewall called and saw people breaking in."

I don't have the energy to twist, or to pull down the visor for the mirror so I can see Jasper. Instead, I close my eyes and inhale, "we were hidden. Unless one of us…"

I don't get to finish that line.

"Not from founding witches," Hawthorne states.

My lids snap open and I find myself staring at the ceiling.

"This town is connected to all in the founding bloodline, and I am bound to this town and Athanasius as part of my punishment. Leo could have been in the area, spying on us."

I turn my head back to the street, wondering if Leo is still out there right now somewhere, and spot Sheriff Wolfe staring our way and shaking his head. "When did he get here?"

"Oh, butterscotch!" Jasper swears. It sounds like swearing.

"You took the words right out of my mouth," Alyssa responds.

Then we watch as Sheriff Wolfe converses with Deputy Huckly, Jaxon Michaels hovering in the doorway.

"He is calling it a prank call," Hawthorne says. "Let's back up and meet with Athanasius about what we found. See what we can work with to get this solved. I am sure Sheriff Wolfe will rip into us later today."

Plans Unfurl

"Hmmmm," Athanasius draws out curiously, bushy white brows scrunched. Even his wrinkles are scrunched. Then he flips a page from the notebook labeled POISONS. "Hmmmm." He flips again and rubs his beard thoughtfully all the way down to his belly. This has gone on several times now.

I guess it is better than hearing the pages rustle over and over in the silence of the shop as we wait for confirmation our actions weren't futile.

"What is 'hmmmm'?" Jasper asks at last, almost sounding like he is mocking the wizard man. But he is anxious. I can see that by how he leans over the desk and shifts his weight repeatedly.

I have to admit, I am quite anxious as well as we have yet to hear from Sheriff Wolfe. It has been a good fifty minutes and we have gone through two notebooks and a folder of polaroid photos. If we were sitting right now, I would be wiggling about and jiggling my legs until all around me are annoyed with my existence.

"Does this answer any questions?" Jasper presses. "Do we have proof?"

I rise onto my toes, lean against the desk, too, and spy over the notebook. Jasper's concern ignites a question of my own. "Or did Alyssa and I just rob a man for nothing and we should prepare to go to jail?" It is likely the files are noticeably gone now.

"I doubt Jaxon Michaels will call in a robbery," Hawthorne interjects from his spot at the right corner of the desk. That seems to be his designated area, where I am not at the moment so he doesn't get a petting from me today. "He would have to explain himself, which wouldn't look good based on what we are seeing before us."

Athanasius pauses at last, stares at the page he is

on, and proceeds to drum his fingers on the desk. He props up his chin with his free hand from there and begins to tap it.

That is different.

"What?" Jasper continues.

"Not all of these are poisonous," Athanasius comments, and he flips another page. "They are all plants, flowers, bushes, trees, berries. Many of them are medicinal, hallucinogenic, ritualistic. Some are deadly, some dangerous, some perfectly safe. I am guessing this notebook started out for poisons because the first five are definitely deadly and specific. After that, however, he started keeping track of everything that can be used in some way, shape, or form." He flips back several pages. "Like this one here." He taps the page.

ANGEL'S TRUMPET.

"This one is actually called brugmansia arborea, which causes severe hallucinations if used improperly or as a poison. It can pull a person completely out of reality. Side effects are also a coma and death. It is the first of many hallucinogens he records, and it is starred in the upper right-hand corner."

"Pull a person out of reality?" I echo, lifting

myself with my arms here until I am dangling over the desk and hovering over the notebook at the same time. I can see the dried plant better now, its description clear below it. It has medicinal purposes, too. That must be what is meant by some way, shape, or form'.

"Wait," Jasper's hand of attention just barely crosses my peripheral. "Does that have any effect on vampires? I always felt like these murders weren't like Doger or Belial. They may love the old ways of feeding, but they are not murderous monsters."

I drop back to the floor, reading deeper into Jasper's question. If Brody was blackmailed, maybe the vampire community was framed. They weren't working together after all.

"Yes," Athanasius replies, flipping to where he was before in the notebook and examining the remaining notes. "It wouldn't be much different except they would need a massively higher dosage for a reaction, like with your antidepressants. It would also wear off quicker, too. Wouldn't kill them, though, as they are not human enough."

"So," I jump in, pointing to the notebook even though the plant is no longer front and center, "that plant could make a vampire, let's say, act on their instincts and attack someone merely out of delirium? Maybe make them think that what they are hunting is an animal rather than a human?"

Athanasius purses his lips and stares up from the notebook as if he needs to think about that. Then he nods. "Yes, I would say so." He directs to Hawthorne here. "Would you agree?"

Hawthorne's whiskers twitch. His tail swishes along papers without sending them flying. "I have never seen it done, but as energy vampires still have a heartbeat (an extremely slow one, but a heartbeat) and blood that flows through them, I would say it is possible."

Energy vampires have a heartbeat? I direct to Jasper, who merely scrunches his features in concern but doesn't look my way. I guess it makes sense with *him* as he is half human. He is even warm to the touch. But a full energy vampire? *Aren't they... dead?*

Undead, my inner voice replies. *And maybe not as dead as a blood vampire. Plus, they are magical.*

I guess that makes sense, but maybe I will ask sometime.

The bell chimes.

"Sounds like Sheriff Wolfe has arrived at last," Athanasius says as he closes the notebook and stacks it with the others. He gathers the photos and gets them into their proper folder.

"Do you think we have something?" I ask.

Athanasius shakes his head. "Not really. You would have to prove these belong to Jaxon Michaels and that he is using them to frame Doger and Belial. Even if you left them in the house, you would have to prove they are there."

"I am thinking I should have convinced you to make an anonymous call," Jasper comments.

"There wasn't really time for that," I reply. "I grabbed, we argued for two seconds, the truck pulled up, and we ran."

"I don't even think an anonymous call would have done much good," Athanasius resumes. "So what? You know Jaxon Michaels keeps notebooks with information that proves he has knowledge about the magical community. But Donald and Linsey are not on the list in the first notebook and there is no sign of the dagger used on Brody. In the end, Jaxon Michaels' memory would simply be wiped, he would be sent far away, these would be confiscated, and that would be that."

"That would be that, huh?"

I don't register the new voice as belonging to Bane, which gets me to spin to the image of the grey-hooded man. The unbearable pain of the dagger plunging into me, into Brody, steals all my senses and I sway a bit as the world around me distorts for a brief time. There I come face to face with Jaxon Michaels. I hadn't really gotten a good look at the guy during the stakeout, but now I see he is just as unkempt as his yard and door hinges. He also already has greying hair, which shows in the stubble around his jaw.

Jaxon Michaels raises a rifle and points it at my chest, his eyes watching me menacingly across the length. The weapon appears so much closer than the shelves several paces away where the possessor of it stands. I swear I can see through the double barrels.

I try to step back, but I forget the desk is as far as I can go and reach up to grab its edge. I am at a loss for what to do next. How to feel. I know I am scared, though, because I have nowhere to run or hide.

"I should thank you for breaking the lockdown

spell, Miss Salem," Jaxon Michaels directs to me in a cool, steady voice that doesn't match his expression. It is like I am seeing two personalities, two faces, of the same man. "It kept my family from acting on all thoughts and desires these past one hundred and twenty-five years. From sharing our knowledge with other humans."

The man's gaze darts to Athanasius and Jasper then, who I am too terrified to look toward as I want to be facing the man who plans to shoot me.

"Oh, yes," Jaxon Michaels proceeds, his voice growing a serpentine tone. "My family retained every bit of memory after the spell locked us away from the rest of the world. We never figured out why just us – maybe it was God's plan, a test of our loyalty. So my family made sure to pass down information and stories from one generation to the next. Each and every family member made sure to take notes of all observations until death. We were determined to never forget but wait out our chance to once and for all destroy your kind. To fulfill our purpose on earth."

Something in me hopes this is some bizarre dream after that rant. It is so end of movie villain, so like the Crucible that I watched not that long ago. I almost let myself believe that, too. Let myself think I fell asleep in the short car ride to the inn to drop off Alyssa. I am good at falling asleep in cars.

Until I hear the gun click into place, the action just below my gaze, and Jaxon Michaels looks back my way. In no dream or nightmare have I ever actually heard a gun click, heard it shoot. In fact, I usually wake up here, then fall back asleep to pick up where I left off.

"Unfortunately, my dear, you don't get a thank you from me because you spoiled my original plan to frame Jasper. I thought it best to expose a half-vampire over a full one, even though Doger and Belial did the killing. The world needs to realize the severity of our demonically run world." That makes him sneer, his cool yet menacing demeanor shifting with ease to disgust. "Humans and demons mating." He spits on the floor. "Humans who choose a demon to love should go to *hell* with them."

I catch Jaxon Michaels' trigger finger twitch, I see him pull back, and I close my eyes. I don't want to face my killer anymore, and it shows in how my heart rises to a level that nearly cripples me. A gasp even escapes.

Then a force rams my side, there is a hiss somehow close by yet far away, the gun goes off, and I hit the floor.

"Get in the storage room!" Athanasius roars in a tone that doesn't fit him.

The hiss comes again as I am ripped off the floor, the sound of another shot going off, and hauled around the desk. I barely have a chance to witness Hawthorne arch, all his fluffiness standing on end, and Athanasius hold his brightly lit staff up high. There is a blue shimmer all around that I do fully note, however, and a clear one that swoops in to join it.

That is when I find myself in the storage room, surrounded by bizarre items.

"Get on the floor," Jasper instructs, shoving me in the direction of the wall. There is a table there with nothing underneath.

Another shot.

I dive under, feeling safer beneath a table than in the open, and Jasper slips in at my side. His arm goes around me. And he feels sticky against my exposed skin. My tank top is riding up.

Next thing I know rounds of bullets are going off

one after the other. Jaxon Michaels is no longer delaying. "Die, wizard! You demonic hell cat!"

I cover my ears, Jasper moving up to help cover me more, and tears spill out and over every inch of my face. I want this all to stop. I want Athanasius and Hawthorne to be all right. I want to go back to the beginning before the murders. I want this to be a nightmare.

"Put the gun down!" enters Sheriff Wolfe's commanding boom. It rolls over the walls and across the floor. "This is your one warning!"

Dramatic laughter as the shooting stops. I can just imagine Jaxon Michaels turning to face Bane in a cocky manner. "You really think I am going to listen to a werewolf?"

Three shots. They are terrifyingly close together and don't sound the same as what rounded off earlier. This sounds more like they are coming from a handgun.

Silence.

"No one move," Sheriff Wolfe continues, just as commanding as when he entered the scene.

I wait. It shouldn't take long from here to know anything. I keep my ears covered the entire time just to make sure, though, as my thoughts wander to what it looks like out there.

"He is dead."

I can't seem to move at that news, however. I am stuck to the floor. But Jasper moves, with a groan, and stumbles backward into one of those bizarre antiques. I hear the thing rock, the stuff behind it tumble to the floor. There I shift my neck to face him and squint. Almost no light fills the storage room.

Jasper is visible enough, though, from the light of the main shop. He is clutching his side and his eyes are closed. His head is leaned back. He looks to be breathing odd.

"Robyn, Jasper," Athanasius calls. "It is safe to come out."

I sit up at last and crawl over. "He is hurt," I respond with a choke of shock. I don't feel fear anymore, just shock. Then I notice the heavy blood stream as I draw closer. A quick glance down shows I am drenched where he touched me.

Shuffling, and Sheriff Wolfe appears at my side before I can even touch my boyfriend. There isn't even a hesitation or moment to ask questions. He simply pushes

Jasper's hands away and presses down on the wound with all he possesses.

Jasper grunts and seethes, throwing his head to the side.

"Sorry," Sheriff Wolfe apologizes. It is here he snaps out his cellphone, the old flip razor phone in red, and presses 3.

I wonder who 3 is and why he isn't using the radio on his shoulder.

That is when Jasper's even stickier fingers graze mine. "Hey," he breathes.

I take his hand and automatically scooch forward a bit more so we are leg to leg.

"Look at you being so brave," Jasper says. "I found me a strong girl."

Sheriff Wolfe mumbles something. I catch the name Sookie and try to listen in, but my attention goes back to Jasper. Only the sense we are not alone tells me that Athanasius and Hawthorne are in the doorway.

"I will be all right," Jasper continues. "Can't kill me that easily."

Sheriff Wolfe's phone snaps closed. "Sam and Sookie will be here soon. They are bringing the cow they plan to use next."

Jasper's lids fail to widen as he shakes his head and directs to the man on his other side. His features turn painfully pleading. "No. I can't. Please. Don't make me."

"You have to, friend," Sheriff Wolfe insists as he shifts to using both hands to press down on Jasper's wound. The blood is flowing fast over his palms and drenching them. "You are bleeding out rapidly. You will die if you don't. I can already see you fading. Feel your body giving out. I have a bad feeling those bullets were poisoned."

The fear returns, this time for Jasper. The shock of the shooting is leaving my system. I can't imagine a life without him.

Just like that I am crying. I am an ugly crier.

"Now look what you have done," Jasper accuses, and it is clear in his voice those words are a struggle. "You scared my girlfriend." He tries to tighten his hold on my hand but it slips in all the wet stickiness, so I do it for him and weasel in at his side.

"If you love her," Sheriff Wolfe resumes quite sternly, "then do as I ask. And know this while you think about it, if you die, I will claim her as mine. I am attracted to her personality and her innocence. I won't hesitate, although I will give her a couple months to mourn. I am not an animal."

Jasper's head glides back my way just as my head rests on his shoulder, revealing his dark eyes already getting hazy, and he reaches for my cheek. His blood smears there, and for once I don't cringe at the thought of being dirty for a while. Heck, my hands are filthy. My clothes and side are filthy. "I will do anything for you. For a first real date with you. *I* want to be the one to take you on your very first date."

I go to reply that I would never ask him to do something that makes him uncomfortable, except...

Jasper completes the distance between us and kisses me gently.

Epilogue

Do I mention at any point how much I hate gatherings?

No? Yes? Don't remember?

Well, I hate them, and again I have no choice but to deal because this is Athanasius I am talking about. Athanasius, who is concerned that I am worrying and wallowing in guilt. So I begrudgingly leave my house with him for My Father's Place.

But everyone is at the diner. Literally. Ev.ry.one.

News travels fast, you see. All who live here should know this by now. So what better place to gather, chitchat, and expand on the official story Bane announced for the sake of the humans in Stars Hollow than My Father's Place. Everyone can move from table to table, eat, have a soda or milkshake.

It's like a party.

It might be a party.

There are definitely new tables and chairs out, enough to hold everyone in the next town over.

Anyway, the story is that Jaxon Michaels, an older man, was interested in the young Linsey. To his dismay, however, an out of towner named Donald Harris usurped her from him. In a rage, he killed them both. Brody witnessed the second murder but failed to get away when he was cornered behind the diner.

As for Doger and Belial, Bane has his pack cleansing their home. For now, the two are staying with family and the humans have no clue about their connection to the murders. They are not being punished as they recall nothing and had no control over their actions.

How Jaxon Michaels got a hold of Jasper's pocket watch and planted it without leaving a trace of himself remains a mystery, however. We can only assume Brody, and possibly Delilah and her family, was involved. Brody has also been placed as the source of the fire in the kitchen, having been the only one in this entire situation to possibly have known about the visions before me and would have had the ability to take action.

Athanasius leads the way to the back, to that perfect table in the far corner. It is the only one available, and there I take a seat with my back to everyone. At least I can be grateful for a spot where I am only surrounded to two sides rather than all four. Here I can send my attention out the window and pretend I am outside and not inside.

That is where I spot Jasper.

Athanasius sighs exasperatedly as he sits across from me. "That young man. He is supposed to be in bed. Particularly as he refused to drain the cow or even get close enough."

Jasper didn't want to be the one to take the cow's life. He even requested that the Thymes not use that cow for whatever future food he orders as he couldn't bear to know the animal he is eating.

I follow Jasper awkwardly from my seat and watch as he comes in, the bell not loud enough to make it over the commotion. He sees us immediately and makes his way over.

"Hey, love," he greets me weakly, hovering over me.

I tilt my head back and he leans over with some struggle to kiss me on the lips.

From there he sits.

Athanasius glares and points a finger. "You, young man, are incorrigible. How did you even get past your father?"

Jasper grins. "He fell asleep watching television, and I was tired of lying around and sleeping." He takes my hand under the table then and we lock eyes.

I don't make eye contact with many people, but Jasper has become an exception.

"Besides, what better medicine than to be with my girl, who held my hand as I did the most excruciating thing in my life."

"Now what is this?" Bane interjects, coming over from the direction of the kitchen. He must have come in the back door. "A party and you didn't invite me?" He claims a seat, and there he takes a second look at Jasper. "Feeling any better?"

Jasper shrugs. "I am still weak. Took me a bit to

walk down the stairs from my apartment, then to make my way across the park."

I redirect back outside to keep my guilt to myself. I wish I could rewind time even further than the start of the murders. I want to go back to the freeway and never walk into this town. Stars Hollow would be better off without me.

"Robyn," Athanasius intrudes into my thoughts. "I told you earlier to stop feeling guilty. None of this is your fault."

I sigh. "Yes, it is. Jaxon Michaels said so himself, although we all knew it from the start. My coming here broke the lockdown spell, which allowed everyone in the world to remember this place. My arrival allowed Jaxon Michaels to attempt to finish what his family started."

Jasper's hand slips out of mine. I am grateful. Maybe he will breakup with me and I won't have a reason to stay. Maybe my exit will reignite the lockdown spell. Except then his arm swoops around me and pulls me and my chair closer until I am against his side.

That gets me to look at the man next to me in disbelief.

"It is not your fault," Jasper agrees. "It is the

world's fault, but it wants you to believe it is you. The world cannot accept what is different, what is special, so chaos is always around the corner waiting to pounce. It is that chaos that we must fight until eventually we all come together as one. This town *is* supposed to represent equality. It was built as a sanctuary. A utopia. A hollow to call home. With your help, we can work to recreate what once was, and maybe from there others will mimic us."

The scratch of a chair. I direct just as Alyssa takes a seat with a flash drive in her possession. "Here," she says, handing the device over to Athanasius. "For you to review. I would like to make it live on Friday."

Athanasius accepts the drive. "I will look it over in the morning."

"Also," Alyssa continues. "I saved Robyn's confrontation with Leo to an external hard drive. It has one terabyte of space. I put it in a safe. All other copies have been deleted. Any new videos of Leo will join it. That way they don't end up in the wrong hands or accidentally get uploaded."

"Thank you," Athanasius replies as he sticks the flash drive in his pocket.

The subject of Leo reminds me of the last encounter with his mother, but I can't just bring her up. Not here, in a packed diner. Not in front of Bane, who technically works for the woman. I will have to take a mental note to bring up that Samantha Stonewall may also be a Dark Witch the next time I am alone with Jasper, Athanasius, and Alyssa.

Sam comes out of the kitchen here, a tray of food balanced on one hand. He sidles up to us and sets a plate before each of us.

"I didn't order," Alyssa remarks, leaning back to give Sam space.

"Sookie expected all of you," Sam replies. "She said it makes sense after all that played out."

And that is how this diner, this table, becomes *our spot*.

Other Publications

Books

The Rogue Beyond the Wall Series

Rogue Beyond the Wall

Tempest of the Rogue

The Sorceress Saga

The King's Sorceress

Journey of the Sorceress

Sorceress Under Siege

Fate of the Sorceress

Sorceress in the Skies

Fiction World: fictional short stories that will take you out of this world

Thoughts of Poetry

Short Stories

An Eclectic Collage published by Freundship Press, LLC

Haunted

Hauntings From the Snake River Plain

Wands Upon a Time

published by Other Bunch Press/River Street Press

    The Blind Man's Dog

Poetry

An Eclectic Collage Vol II: Relationships of Life published by Freundship Press, LLC

    Sea of Love

    Memory

An Eclectic Collage Vol IV: For the Love of Animals published by Freundship Press, LLC

    Chuck-It

    Thoughts of a Senior Cat

Wands Upon a Time

Printed in Great Britain
by Amazon